**'I won't be w...**
**week—unless...**
**home with Sop...**

Sophie would adore... ...ly all to herself—and maybe nursing his daughter through her illness was the wake-up call Oliver needed. The thing that would make him start concentrating on his family. Though Rachel already knew what his reaction was going to be.

'No, she needs her mum with her.'

Sophie needed her dad, too. So did Robin. But Rachel wasn't feeling up to a row. 'If you think it's best,' she said coolly.

Oliver raked a hand through his dark hair. 'Don't worry. I'll sort things out at the practice.'

Hell. Why did he have to look so *sexy* when she didn't have time to do anything about it? Since they'd had the children they didn't spend Sunday mornings in bed any more. Rachel realised just how much she missed it—the warmth of her husband's body heating hers, tangled limbs, the roughness of the hairs on his chest against her skin.

Then she remembered last night. The guilt-gift—chocolates that she hadn't been able to face eating because she knew why he'd bought them and they would have stuck in her throat…

**Kate Hardy** lives on the outskirts of Norwich with her husband, two small children, two lazy spaniels—and too many books to count! She wrote her first book at age six, when her parents gave her a typewriter for her birthday. She had the first of a series of sexy romances published at twenty-five, and swapped a job in marketing communications for freelance health journalism when her son was born so she could spend more time with him. She's wanted to write for Mills & Boon® since she was twelve—and when she was pregnant with her daughter her husband pointed out that writing Medical Romances™ would be the perfect way to combine her interest in health issues with her love of good stories. It really is the best of both worlds—especially as she gets to meet a new gorgeous hero every time... Kate is always delighted to hear from readers—do drop in to her website at www.katehardy.com

**Recent books by the same author:**

THE DOCTOR'S PREGNANCY SURPRISE*
THE BABY DOCTOR'S DESIRE*
THE DOCTOR'S TENDER SECRET*
THE REGISTRAR'S CONVENIENT WIFE
THE SPANISH CONSULTANT'S BABY

*London City General trilogy

# THEIR
# VERY SPECIAL
# MARRIAGE

BY
KATE HARDY

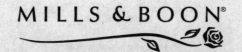

MILLS & BOON®

For Gay—my much-loved stepmother

*All the characters in this book have no existence outside the imagination
of the author, and have no relation whatsoever to anyone bearing the
same name or names. They are not even distantly inspired by any
individual known or unknown to the author, and all the incidents are
pure invention.*

*First published in Great Britain 2005
Harlequin Mills & Boon Limited,
Eton House, 18-24 Paradise Road, Richmond, Surrey TW9 1SR*

© Pamela Brooks 2005

ISBN 0 263 84311 4

*Set in Times Roman 10½ on 11½ pt.
03-0605-50123*

*Printed and bound in Spain
by Litografia Rosés, S.A., Barcelona*

# CHAPTER ONE

THE noise was deafening. Thirty children running around in the huge room, crawling through tunnels, sliding down enormous tubes into a pool of brightly coloured balls, jumping harder and harder on the bouncy castle until—

Rachel saw it happening from the other side of the room, but she wasn't fast enough to get there in time to stop it. Robin misjudged his bounce, moved at the wrong angle and clashed heads with one of his classmates. Rachel raced towards them, but Oliver was already there. Both little boys were crying and holding their heads, and he led them away from the bouncy castle to a quieter corner of the room.

'All right, let's have a look at you, birthday boy.' His gentle, teasing tone helped to soothe the little boy. 'Robin, can you tell Daddy where it hurts?' He gently checked the little boy. His fingers probed the bump to help him estimate the extent of the injury, then he checked the little boy's pupils. Robin was still crying, but Oliver kissed his forehead, stroked his hair and turned to the other little boy, who was holding one hand to his forehead and crying equally hard.

By the time Rachel brought over two cold pads—years of working together meant that Oliver hadn't needed to ask her for them—both little boys had stopped sobbing.

'Here we go. Let's put a cold compress on to make you feel better,' Rachel said. 'Do you two want to come and sit with me for a little while and have a story?'

Two small, solemn heads nodded.

'Come on, then.' Rachel moved so the boys could both

sit on her knee, and her gaze met Oliver's for a moment. His wry smile said it all: *Kids*.

'Pupils both equal and reactive, for both of them,' he said softly. 'No signs of loss of consciousness, though I think Mikey's going to have a bit of a shiner.'

She nodded. But with head injuries, you couldn't be too careful—what looked like a harmless bump could turn into something nasty a few hours later. A tear in an artery could lead to an extradural haemorrhage, where blood pooled between the bone and the dura and caused pressure inside the skull to rise. They'd need to keep a close eye on Robin—in case he started being sick, had a severe headache or fits—and warn Mikey's parents to do the same.

That was the one bad thing about being a qualified doctor: you knew the worst-case scenario. And when your own children were involved, you stopped being rational and calm and remembered the rarest complications of any condition.

Oliver was smiling at her now, and Rachel was conscious of a jolt somewhere in the region of her heart. Even after fourteen years of being together—eight years of marriage—her husband's smile could still make her heart turn over. Just the curve of his mouth, and remembering the pleasure that mouth had brought to her over the years. Or the light in his blue, blue eyes. He'd smiled at her like that at Robin's second birthday party and, nine months later, Sophie had made her arrival into the world.

Would they make love tonight?

Oh, now she was really getting depraved. Thinking about sex in the middle of a six-year-old's birthday party. But it had been a while. Oliver had been too busy, Rachel had been too tired, and the weeks had slipped by. Maybe tonight she should make an effort. When Rob and Sophie were asleep, she'd put some chilling-out music on the CD player, open a bottle of wine and tempt Oliver to relax with her.

'That's my daddy,' she heard Sophie lisp proudly. 'He makes people better. So does my mummy.'

'Come on, little one. Shall we go and tell the ladies we're nearly ready for tea and Robin's birthday cake?' Oliver asked, picking up his daughter and lifting her onto his shoulders.

Rachel smiled gratefully at him. 'Thanks, love,' she mouthed, and started telling her son and his best friend a complicated story about pirates and dragons which soon had them forgetting their bump on the bouncy castle.

After the birthday tea—where all the healthy options of raisins, cherry tomatoes and cubes of cheese were ignored in favour of crisps and chocolate finger biscuits, and the jelly and ice cream disappeared in record time—and two rousing choruses of 'Happy Birthday to You', because Sophie wanted to be like her big brother and blow out the candles, too, the children dispersed, clutching a balloon, a windmill and a party bag. Rachel strapped the children into their car seats while Oliver paid for the party and brought Robin's pile of presents back to the car.

'Did you have a nice party, darling?' she asked Robin.

'It was brilliant!' Robin's smile was a mile wide.

'Can we have another one next week?' Sophie asked.

Rachel laughed. 'We'll have to wait until it's your birthday, Soph.'

'But that's *ages* away,' Robin said in dismay.

'Never mind. We can try out your new bike when we get home,' Rachel suggested, knowing it would distract him.

The ploy worked, because Robin started chattering about his new bike and how it had got proper gears and a really loud bell.

'And I can go on my pink scooter,' Sophie said. 'Robin, you've got to wear your hat.' She blew on her windmill. 'Look, Daddy, it goes round!'

'Mmm.'

Oliver was making the right noises but Rachel could hear that his heart definitely wasn't in it. She shot him a sideways look and groaned inwardly. She knew that look. He was thinking about the practice.

Today was their son's birthday. His sixth birthday. Oliver had swapped duties so he wasn't on morning surgery or on call. He'd *promised* to spend the day with them as a family. To give him his due, he'd spent the day with them so far. He'd been good with the kids at the party, chatted to the other parents. But Rachel knew it just wasn't possible for Oliver Bedingfield to go for more than four hours without thinking about the practice.

So she was prepared for her husband to check his mobile phone as soon as they got indoors, and equally prepared for the apologetic look on his face.

'Sorry, love. There's something I need to sort out.'

Couldn't he put the children—and her—first, for once? But no. He was a Bedingfield, brought up to believe that his duty to the community came before everything else. 'Rob wanted to show you how good he is on his bike,' she reminded him. She'd taken the stabilisers off Robin's old bike a week ago to get him prepared for his birthday present. Where she'd grown up, it was always the dads who taught their kids how to ride a bike. In the Kent village where they lived, even, it was the dads who did the bike-riding lessons.

Except for Oliver.

'I'll come and see him ride it later. I promise,' Oliver said.

His eyes had grown wary, as if he was expecting a row. He damned well deserved one, Rachel thought angrily. Was one single day too much to ask?

Clearly, it was. She forced herself to smile at him, even though she wanted to shake him and tell him their kids were growing up so fast and he was missing everything—that he wouldn't get this time back again and he was *wasting* it. 'OK. We'll be out in the front garden.'

'I'll be with you as soon as I can,' Oliver said.

But he didn't meet her eyes, and when he walked into his office in the house Rachel knew he wouldn't come out into the front garden with them. He never did. She was always the one who watched the children when they went out to play, chatted to other parents in the street.

It wasn't that Oliver was a snob. He was good with people and everyone in the village loved their GP. But his background was so different from Rachel's own. He'd grown up in the big house at the far end of the village, always that little bit apart from the others; she'd grown up on an estate in Newcastle where everyone popped in and out of each other's houses, and children went from garden to garden, playing noisy and busy games until somebody's mum came out with a tray of orange squash and biscuits. When she'd been pregnant with Rob and they'd moved to the small modern estate on the edge of the village, she'd thought that Oliver would fit in and discover what it meant to live right in the middle of a close community. That he'd break away from the Bedingfield way of doing things.

But then Oliver's father decided to retire, over a long enough period for Oliver to ease into taking his place as the senior partner in the practice. So Oliver didn't get the time to join in with Rachel. And, following the Bedingfield tradition, he always kept slightly apart from everyone else.

If it hadn't been for that clash of heads and the fact that his medical expertise had been needed, he'd have stayed remote at the party, too. On the sidelines, making all the right noises, but his mind elsewhere. Sometimes Rachel thought she was on the way to losing the man she'd fallen in love with, because Oliver was turning into his father. He even ran the practice along the same lines as Stuart Bedingfield had. But this was the twenty-first century—nobody doffed their cap to the village bank manager, solicitor or doctor any more. It was time to let the old ways go, forget the social niceties that were no longer an issue.

'Penny for them?'

Rachel jumped. She'd been lost in her thoughts, watching the children at the same time. 'Just thinking how quickly they grow up,' she lied. Much as she liked her neighbour, Ginny, she couldn't talk to her about Oliver. The last thing she wanted was rumours floating round the village that all wasn't well between Oliver and Rachel Bedingfield.

'Don't they just? I remember when Jack was six. It seems like yesterday—and now he's eleven and nearly as tall as me! Did Rob enjoy his party?'

'Loved it.' Rachel grinned. 'Funny, you'd think that two hours at Bounce would wear them out. But he'll be zooming round on that bike until it's dark.'

'Ah, bless.' Ginny gave her a curious look. 'Oliver working, is he?'

So even the neighbours had noticed. Great. She shrugged. 'Something cropped up.'

'Your life's not your own when you're the village doctor,' Ginny said. 'You must get it, too—people coming up to you at nursery or in the playground to ask you "just a quick question".'

Parents only did that so they didn't have to risk facing the practice's dragon secretary if they didn't have the luck to get Rita, the receptionist, to ask for an appointment to see Rachel. Another sticking point, another battle that Rachel knew she'd never win. But when Prunella eventually retired, Rachel was going to make sure Oliver didn't hire a carbon copy as her replacement. 'Better them grab me in the street than have them worrying about the kids,' Rachel said, and deftly changed the subject.

Oliver still hadn't joined them by the time it was too dark

for the children to play outside safely. Rachel shepherded Robin and Sophie indoors. 'Do you want anything to eat?'

'I'm stuffed,' Robin said.

'I'm stuffed, too,' Sophie said, not to be outdone.

'Milk, bath and bed, I think,' Rachel said.

'But Daddy didn't see me on my bike,' Robin protested.

Rachel gave him a hug. 'He'll see you on your bike tomorrow, love.'

'He'll be busy,' Sophie said.

Hell. If even a three-year-old spotted that her father didn't spend enough time with them—and made excuses for him—then it was time to do something.

What, Rachel wasn't sure. She pulled her weight at the surgery, as did the other doctors and the practice nurse. Maybe she should persuade Oliver to get a practice manager to take the admin burden off him. But it had been the Bedingfield practice for so long…she had a feeling he'd resist. If he didn't, his family would. The Bedingfields were a sensitive lot and it would be all too easy to start a full-scale family feud. She really didn't need to give them an extra excuse to dislike her. Being forthright and Northern was more than enough for them. She had to go carefully.

As usual, bathtime meant there was more water on the floor than in the bath. Rachel dried the children and mopped up. 'Teeth, story, bed,' she said.

'But it's my birthday,' Robin protested.

'You know the routine. Teeth, story, bed.'

'A princess story?' Sophie asked, beaming.

Rachel hid a smile. Sophie and her 'pwintheth thtorieth'. Not that Oliver would have got the joke. He didn't do bedtime routines. Didn't have time. Just the same as it was always Rachel who helped Rob do his homework and make birthday cards, Rachel who'd taught both children their letters and colours and numbers, Rachel who listened to Robin's reading, Rachel who did all the liaison with the school, Rachel who did the laundry and the packed lunches. 'OK, you can choose a princess story. Rob, you can read whatever story you like, but no more than twenty minutes, OK?'

'I'll kiss Daddy goodnight.' Before Rachel could stop her, Sophie had rushed down the stairs and flung open the door to Oliver's office. 'Daddy!'

'Come on, Rob. Come and have a birthday kiss, too,' Rachel said.

Oliver definitely wasn't pleased at the interruption. He was trying to hide it in front of the children, but she recognised the little furrow between his eyebrows. A furrow that was actually starting to leave a line, it appeared so frequently nowadays.

'Daddy, Daddy.' Sophie climbed onto her father's lap and hugged him. 'Love you.' Then she leaned backwards and put one hand out to steady herself. It landed on the keyboard of Oliver's computer.

There was a loud beep and Oliver's mouth tightened. 'You've deleted the file,' he said between clenched teeth.

Rachel hastily scooped Sophie out of Oliver's arms. 'It was an accident. She's three, Oliver,' she reminded him. 'And you can always restore the file.'

'No, because I hadn't saved it. I've lost the last half-hour's work.'

'The system's got an autosave function,' she reminded him, her eyes narrowing.

Robin was hanging back by the doorway, looking worried. Rachel sighed inwardly. 'Are you going to give the birthday boy a bedtime kiss?' she asked Oliver quietly.

'Of course.' Oliver opened his arms stiffly. ''Night, Robin. And happy birthday.'

Not as happy as it *had* been. Not as happy as it could have been. Sometimes, Rachel thought, she could murder her husband. Why couldn't he put himself in the kids' shoes just occasionally?

She shepherded the children to bed, read Sophie three stories about Princess Mouse, let Robin finish the chapter of his book about the robot dog, then kissed them both goodnight and turned off the lights.

Now for Oliver.

'Don't make it into a confrontation,' she reminded herself quietly as she walked downstairs. 'You'll just set his back up and get nowhere. If you want him to listen and do something positive, take it softly.' She rapped on the door of his office and put her head round the door. 'Oliver?'

He glanced up.

'Did you get your file sorted?'

'No, thanks to Sophie. Rachel, you know I don't like the children coming in here.'

They wouldn't *have* to go in if he'd come out to them! She bit back her irritation. 'Oliver, your memory's fantastic—it won't take you that long to put it back together.' She paused. '*Saltimbocca* OK for dinner?' His favourite. That would put him in a good mood, surely?

He shook his head. 'Thanks, but I'm not that hungry. Besides, I've got a lot to do—as well as making up on that half-hour's work I lost.'

Which had been an *accident*. And it was only a computer file, hardly a life-or-death situation. She took a deep breath. If she pushed it now, they'd have a row. 'I'll make you a sandwich. But, Oliver…I think we need to talk.'

'About what?'

Did he really not know? Did he think this was a *normal* marriage? Then again, it might well be, in his terms. He was probably following his father's pattern. 'About us.'

'We're all right.'

He sounded so sure. Maybe he was right. Maybe the problem was all in her head. Rachel didn't have the energy for a row. She gave up. 'Do you want a glass of wine with your sandwich?'

He shook his head. 'I'm fine, thanks.'

She made a sandwich and quietly took it through to his office. He mumbled a thank you, but she knew he hardly saw her. Her own sandwich tasted like ashes and most of it ended up in the bin. When was the last time they'd eaten as a family? Or was she simply expecting too much?

When she checked on the children, Robin was clutching his favourite teddy in one hand and the string to a rocket-shaped helium balloon—the one her mother had sent by special delivery that morning—in the other. Gently, she disentangled the string and put it safely at the side of the room. He murmured in his sleep; she stroked his hair. 'Goodnight, Rob. Sweet dreams. I love you,' she whispered.

Sophie was lying like a small baby with her forearms flopped back, her hands by her ears. Her duvet was half over her face. Rachel straightened it and stroked her daughter's hair. 'Goodnight, Soph. Sweet dreams. I love you,' she said softly.

Her beautiful children. Both with Oliver's straight dark hair and china-blue eyes. Rob had Oliver's half-shy smile and tended to keep on the edge of things; Sophie was confident and was usually in the middle. Usually in charge, Rachel thought with a smile. She'd have to teach Sophie to curb her bossy tendencies.

Her smile faded. Oliver wouldn't. He probably hadn't even noticed.

She shook herself. Stop feeling so sorry for yourself, Rachel Bedingfield, she told herself harshly. You've got a good marriage, a good man and two fabulous children. You've got a job you love, a nice house and no financial worries. What have you got to be miserable about? Pull yourself together!

Maybe a bath would help. Preferably shared with Oliver—

they just about fitted into the bath together—but she knew that was asking for too much. The mood he was in, he'd snap at her if she suggested it.

She used the expensive bath foam he'd bought her for Christmas, and settled back with a magazine.

*Is your husband cheating on you? Check our ten typical signs.*

She rolled her eyes. Oliver wasn't a cheat. He didn't have time to do anything but work. All the same, she couldn't help reading it and answering the questions in her head.

*His looks.*

Ha. He hadn't changed there. Not the way he dressed, the toiletries he used. Definitely not.

*His work…an excuse to account for time spent away.*

The back of Rachel's neck prickled. She shook herself. Of course not. Oliver was just a workaholic. He always had been, even as a student.

*Personality or behavioural changes.*

Hmm. He'd become withdrawn and distant, but that was to do with work—wasn't it? Rachel looked closer at the section. *They may be subtle and gradual.* Um. When had Oliver started being distant? *Your spouse may be touchy— reflecting the effort of keeping the affair hidden, the fear of discovery and guilt.* No. Of course not. He was just touchy because he was working too hard.

*Telephone tip-offs.*

She hadn't had any odd calls, nobody hanging up as soon as she answered. Sure, Oliver checked his mobile phone a lot, but that was work.

*Sex.*

Changes in your sex life. Ha. What sex life? She couldn't remember the last time they'd made love. She swallowed. Was that because he was doing it with somebody else? No. Of course not. It was work again. Work, and she was often tired from looking after the children in between doing her shifts at the surgery. He was tired, too, because he put in long hours. It was just a phase their marriage was going through. It happened to every couple from time to time…didn't it?

*Computer use.*

An online or cyber-affair. No. He didn't hide his files when anyone walked into his office. He just didn't like being disturbed when he was working. That little nagging voice in the back of her head was completely wrong.

*Changes in habits.*

Ha. Well, he wasn't doing that. He didn't have time to go to the gym and his taste in music hadn't changed recently. As for what he ate… Tonight, when he hadn't wanted her to cook for them, he'd just been tired and busy.

*Gifts.*

Hmm. Well, she hadn't noticed any gifts or receipts hanging about. He hadn't been buying her things out of guilt either. Cross that one off.

*Closed doors.*

As a way of distancing himself, physically and emotionally? Hmm. Well, it was only his office door that he kept closed. Work again.

*Friends and family notice discord between you.*

Ginny's comment had only been about Oliver's workaholic habits. Hadn't it?

All the same, Rachel couldn't help noticing how many of the signs applied. Seven out of ten. Which she'd blamed on work.

*A sexually, emotionally or physically absent partner is likely to be getting fulfilment somewhere else.*

No, no and no. She was just being paranoid. Stupid. It was only an article in a magazine. It didn't mean that Oliver was having an affair. She closed the magazine and dunked it in the bath. 'So there,' she said.

But there was an empty feeling in her heart as she climbed out and dried herself. And an even emptier feeling as she went to bed. Alone.

## CHAPTER TWO

OLIVER blinked hard. His eyes were sore from the time he'd spent at the computer. But every time he'd thought about stopping, he'd heard his father's voice. *I'm relying on you, son. Keep the practice going, just as I would.*

How could he let his father down? Nigel had dropped out of medicine after the third year, which had left Oliver as the one who had to keep the family practice going. Sometimes, just sometimes, Oliver wished his elder brother would shoulder his share of the family responsibilities. But he was realistic enough to know Nigel never would, and their mother would always have a ready excuse for him. Which left Oliver to carry the burden on his own.

The house was completely silent. Oliver couldn't even hear Squeak, the family hamster, running on his wheel. With a sigh he checked that the doors were locked, and trudged upstairs to the bedroom. Rachel's bedside light was still on, but she was asleep.

It was barely half past ten.

Couldn't she have waited up for him for once? She knew how busy he was, that he had to put the hours in at his desk at home. He was senior partner at the practice. He had *responsibilities*, to his patients as well as to his family. But Rachel always seemed to have an early night nowadays. Leaving him to unwind on his own in front of the news, sport or a film he didn't really want to see.

He stripped and had a shower, half hoping that the sound of the water would wake her. Maybe she'd surprise him, open the shower door and slide in next to him, and...

Oh, who was he trying to kid? He couldn't remember the

last time they'd made love. Every time he made an overture, she gave him that apologetic little smile. 'Sorry, love. I'm a bit tired. Maybe tomorrow night?'

And tomorrow never came.

So, lately, he'd stopped even asking. There wasn't any point.

OK, to be fair, Rachel worked long hours, too. She did her shifts at the surgery, kept the house running, looked after the children. Oliver was guiltily aware that he didn't do as much as he should on the parenting front, that he'd used work to duck his responsibilities at home. But Rachel was so much better at that sort of thing than he was. She always knew how to make things right when the kids were upset.

He just wished she could make *him* feel better.

His mouth tightened as he towelled himself dry. And what had that been about earlier this evening? *We need to talk. About us.* Was she…?

No, of course not. They were all right. It was just a phase that most couples with small kids went through. He'd seen enough of them in his surgery, women tired out by child care and feeling neglected by their spouses.

Maybe he'd buy Rachel some flowers tomorrow. Show her he appreciated her. And then maybe she'd show him some appreciation, too. And if she didn't appreciate him…well, at least there was one person who did. One person he could talk to. And maybe *she* could shed some light on what was going on in Rachel's head.

Rachel was already up the next morning when Oliver woke. He could hear her in the bathroom, cleaning Sophie's teeth and encouraging Robin to clean his. By the time Oliver had showered, dressed and gone downstairs, the children were ready for school and Rachel had set a cafetière of coffee next to his place at the kitchen table.

'See you at the surgery,' she said. 'Soph, Rob, give Daddy a kiss goodbye.'

'Love you, Daddy,' they both said.

Oliver hugged them back. 'Love you, too. Have a nice day at school.'

'Nursery, Daddy,' Sophie corrected him. 'I'm going to big school *next* year.'

He couldn't help grinning. His daughter was so pedantic. But she had her mother's smile, wide and welcoming, enough to charm anyone. And that cute little lisp meant she could get away with murder. 'All right, Sophie. Nursery, then.'

She nodded in satisfaction. 'Bye, Daddy.'

'Bye,' Rob echoed.

'Bye.' Rachel leaned over and kissed him on the cheek.

Oliver was almost tempted to grab her and kiss her properly. But then she'd be late dropping the kids off and her surgery would start late, so she'd be late picking Sophie up from nursery again and…oh, it would be just too much hassle. He contented himself with a 'See you later'. She gave him an odd look, but he shrugged it off. Rachel was just in a funny mood right now. Probably PMT. He'd go carefully for the next couple of days, and then she'd be back to her usual sunny self. He hoped.

When Rachel had dropped Sophie at nursery and Robin at school, she drove to the surgery. Her first patient, Teresa Lord, was already waiting for her.

'What can I do for you, Teresa?' she asked with a smile.

'It's…' Teresa sighed. 'I know this is going to sound stupid. But I've been so miserable, and my sister's taking Prozac. She says it makes you feel so much brighter. And I wondered…'

Rachel's heart sank. She hated it when patients thought antidepressants were the answer to everything. 'It's one of several options, yes,' Rachel said carefully. 'So how have you been feeling?'

'Low.'

'How are you sleeping?' Waking early—often two or three hours earlier than usual—was a common symptom of depression.

'OK. It's just it's a bit hard to get to sleep.' Teresa bit her lip. 'I lie there and think.'

'Is anything particular bothering you?' Rachel asked gently.

'No.' Teresa sighed and her shoulders sagged. 'Yes.'

'Tell me about it. Maybe I can help,' Rachel offered.

Teresa looked torn between wanting to confide and afraid that it would make things worse. Rachel had a fair idea why her patient was worried. 'Remember, whatever you tell me is confidential. I'm your doctor. I'm not going to gossip about you in the playground. Nobody in the village will hear a word from me,' she said quietly. Teresa's face cleared, and Rachel knew she'd guessed correctly. She waited, knowing that it was best to let the patient set the pace.

'It's my husband,' Teresa blurted out. 'I think he's having an affair.'

Ouch. Just what Rachel had half been thinking about Oliver. 'What makes you think that?'

'He's been distant with me lately. And he's working late every night. And he snaps at me and the kids. Then he can be so loving… I thought maybe he was worried about something at work. But then I read this article, and I recognised the signs.'

You and me both, Rachel thought grimly. I bet you read the same article I did. 'Just because you did a quiz in a magazine and the results weren't very nice, it doesn't mean Dick's definitely having an affair,' she reassured Teresa, though she was sure her words sounded hollow. 'You'd be much better off talking to him about your worries. The longer you leave it, the more anxious you're going to get, the worse you'll feel and the more likely you are to end up having a hell of a row instead of discussing it calmly.'

'So you're not going to give me antidepressants?'

'Antidepressants can be useful in cases of clinical depression—they change the chemicals in your brain,' Rachel said. 'But I think in your case, Teresa, they're not going to help. You're upset for a reason—a good reason—and the way to help yourself feel better again is to tackle the cause of what you're worrying about. If you don't want to talk to Dick about it on your own, talking to a counsellor's a good start. It'll help you find some common ground with him.'

'I don't know if he'll agree to go.'

Mmm. Rachel could dish out the advice, but she couldn't take it herself. If she asked Oliver to go to marriage counselling with her, he'd probably look at her as if she'd grown three heads. 'Then why don't you get your mum to have the kids for the night, sit down with Dick and talk things through with him? If you tell him how you're feeling and listen to how he's feeling, too, you might be able to see a way through it together. It might be that he's got problems at work, he doesn't want to worry you about them, and he doesn't realise how he's being at home.'

'Or he might be having an affair,' Teresa said glumly.

'If he is, then taking antidepressants isn't going to change anything. You need to talk to each other,' Rachel said gently. She looked up the numbers for the nearest counsellors on her computer, wrote three of them down and handed the paper to Teresa. 'Before you talk to him, you could have a word with one of these. They can give you some tips to help you discuss things without making it a confrontation.'

'I suppose.'

Rachel reached over and squeezed Teresa's hand. 'You might be getting yourself worked up about nothing. Give it a try. You can always come back and see me again if it doesn't help and you're still feeling low.'

'What about St John's wort? My cousin takes that.'

'Some studies show it's effective with depression,' Rachel said. 'But it reacts with some medications—it makes the drugs go through the body too quickly so they don't work properly. The Pill's one of the drugs it reacts with, so if you're going to take St John's wort you'll need to use an extra method of contraception.'

'I never thought of that,' Teresa said, blinking in surprise. 'It's a natural remedy. I just assumed it'd be safe to take.'

'It can be, if you're not taking any other medications,' Rachel said. 'But if you do go into the chemist for a complementary remedy, it's always worth having a chat with the pharmacist before you buy it, just to check it's going to suit you and won't interfere with anything else you're taking—and also how long you should take it for.'

Teresa nodded. 'Thanks, Rachel.'

Rachel smiled back. 'That's what I'm here for.'

When Teresa left, Rachel waited a while before buzzing her next patient in. Teresa's worries had made her own doubts resurface. Supposing Oliver *was* having an affair? Would he agree to see a relationship counsellor? Or would the suggestion be the thing to push him over the edge and make him leave her?

She shook herself. Ridiculous. They had a strong marriage. They'd been together for fourteen years, despite the initial opposition of his family. Two gorgeous children. Oliver wouldn't walk out on them…would he?

Oliver buzzed his first patient in. 'Good morning, Mrs Porter. How are you?'

'Fine. Well, um, look, I don't want to waste your time, Dr Bedingfield. It's a bit silly.'

'That's what I'm here for,' Oliver said with a smile. 'What's the problem?'

'I keep getting pins and needles in my hand. I've been waking up in the night and my hand's just numb until I shake it or rub it.'

'Do you get it during the day as well?'

'Not really. It's a lot worse at night,' Hayley said.

'It sounds as if it might be carpal tunnel syndrome,' Oliver said. 'The bones in your wrist form a tunnel, called the carpal tunnel, and the main nerve in your hand—the median nerve—goes through it, together with other tendons and ligaments. When the tendons get swollen for any reason, they squash the median nerve and that's what causes the pain and tingling. May I take a look at your hand?'

'It's the left one.' She held it out for inspection.

'Does it affect your fingers at all?'

'My thumb, first finger and middle finger,' she said.

A textbook case—but he needed to check a couple of things. 'OK. I'm going to ask you to do a couple of things which will tell me where the problem is.' He started with Tinel's test—tapping over the carpal tunnel in the wrist to see if he could reproduce the tingling. 'How does that feel?'

'My fingers are tingling,' Hayley admitted.

Positive: so next he'd try Phalen's test. 'I want you to flex your wrist for me, as hard as you can.' He smiled as she followed his instructions. 'Yes, that's perfect.' He kept half an eye on the second hand of the clock as he spoke. 'Have you ever had pins and needles in your hand before?'

'A bit, when I was pregnant.'

He nodded. Rachel would probably know about that. She did all the antenatal appointments at the practice. 'You often get carpel tunnel syndrome in the last few months of pregnancy.'

'That's what Rachel said.'

Rachel, not 'Dr Bedingfield', he noticed. Rachel's style

of medicine was very different from his own. 'Is there a possibility you're pregnant at the moment?'

Hayley shook her head. 'Definitely not.'

There were other medical conditions which affected the carpal tunnel, too, including wrist fractures, diabetes, thyroid disease and rheumatoid arthritis. Repeating the same hand movements over and over again could cause it—it was common with people who used computers, assembly-line workers and mechanics and people who played a lot of golf or did a lot of gardening. 'Have you changed your job lately, or taken up a new hobby, or texted people more than usual on your mobile phone?'

'I started doing cross-stitch last month,' Hayley said. 'But would that cause it?'

'It's a repetitive hand movement so, yes, it could be part of the problem,' Oliver said.

'But I use my right hand for stitching.'

'And the left for holding an embroidery ring?'

'Well, yes.' Hayley grimaced. 'My hand's tingling now.'

'OK, you can relax your hand.' He noticed that she flicked her wrist to stop the pins and needles: a characteristic response to carpal tunnel syndrome.

'What we can start with is a wrist splint at night—that will stop your wrist from moving, but you'll be able to do pretty much anything you usually do with your hands. Taking some ibuprofen at night, just before you go to bed, can help with the inflammation. You also need to change the way you do needlework—take more breaks, so it gives your wrist and hand a chance to rest. If that doesn't work, there are a couple of other things we can try.'

'What sort of things?'

'An injection of corticosteroids into your wrist often helps.'

She shook her head. 'I'm not good with needles.'

'The other option's minor surgery to release the pressure on the nerve.'

'You mean, cut my wrist open?'

'It'll stop the pain and you'll get full use of your hand and wrist back within a couple of months.'

Hayley grimaced. 'I think I'd rather put up with the pins and needles!'

'Hopefully it won't come to that. I'll prescribe you a splint and Rosie—' the practice nurse '—can show you how to put it on. Give it six weeks—around three in four patients find it's a lot better then. If it's not any better, come back and have a chat with me.'

'And have an injection?'

'Not necessarily. I mean have a chat, see how you're feeling and discuss what your options are. I promise, no needles unless that's what you decide you want.'

She almost sagged in relief. 'Thanks, Dr Bedingfield.'

'Pleasure.'

The rest of morning surgery flew by, and Oliver definitely needed a cup of coffee at the end of it. Rachel was already in the rest room. He sighed inwardly, hoping that the tension between them from last night would have vanished, but half expecting it would still be there.

'Hello.'

She spun round and smiled when she saw him. 'Hi.' She added milk to the mug of coffee she'd just poured and handed it to him.

Peace offering? He just about stopped himself uttering the words. 'Thanks.'

'Had a good morning?' she asked as she made a second mug of coffee.

'Average. Though I had a nasty case of carpal tunnel. Hayley Porter.'

'Mmm, she had it when she was pregnant,' Rachel said. 'Poor thing. It's still giving her gyp, then?'

'I've given her a wrist splint, and told her to take ibuprofen before bed. Hopefully that'll help. If not, the next step's a steroid injection.'

'Which could itself cause problems—apart from making sure you don't touch the median nerve when you put the needle in, there's a risk of the patient developing a haematoma,' Rachel said. 'Plus she might need a second injection and splints if it doesn't work. And if *that* doesn't work, you'll have to divide the flexor retinaculum to decompress the nerve.'

'We can do it by keyhole surgery,' Oliver said.

She shook her head. 'I know endoscopic techniques—' keyhole surgery '—mean that patients recover faster, but there's less risk of a complication with the open technique, and more chance that you'll release the carpal tunnel fully. Half the time with endoscopic techniques you can't see well enough and you have to convert it to an open technique anyway.'

His turn for a peace offering. 'Want me to refer her to you?' He knew Rachel didn't get to do as much minor surgery as she'd like.

Rachel nodded. 'Please. Not that you're a bad doctor. She's just really, really scared of needles. Lucy—' the midwife for Hollybridge and the next village '—gave up in the end and sent her to me to do the antenatal blood tests.'

'Then you'd be the best doctor to calm her down. She's used to you and she trusts you.'

'She trusts *you*, Oliver. Everyone does.'

Did they? He wasn't so sure. Especially where his wife was concerned. 'Rach, what you were saying yesterday...'

'Hmm?'

'About us. I've been thinking.'

She looked nervous; her brown eyes suddenly went very, very dark. 'What about us?'

'You've got a point. We don't ever talk about us any more, only about work or the children.'

She nodded. 'Maybe we should—'

But before she could finish, Rita, the practice receptionist, put her head round the door. 'Rachel, sorry to interrupt, I've got the hospital on the phone. Says it's urgent.'

'Hell. I'm expecting some test results. If they're calling, that means bad news,' she said. She gave Oliver an apologetic smile. 'Sorry, I really need to take that call. Catch you later?'

'Sure.'

Though he couldn't help wondering. What had she been about to suggest? He had no idea. He didn't know what Rachel was thinking a lot of the time nowadays. Maybe they could try again and talk tonight when the kids were in bed.

Maybe.

# CHAPTER THREE

EXCEPT things didn't work out quite as Oliver planned. Surgery overran and the florist was closed when he got there, so he had to make do with what was left at the supermarket. Not the ideal choice, but the thought was what counted, wasn't it?

'Thank you,' Rachel said politely when he handed her the huge bunch of carnations. Then she gave him a suspicious look. 'What are they for?'

What did she mean? He'd bought them because he knew she liked flowers. 'Do I need an excuse to buy my wife flowers?' he demanded.

'No-o.'

But she didn't sound that sure. He tried to remember when he'd last bought her flowers—except for birthdays and anniversaries—and drew a blank. Hell. No wonder she looked leery. She probably thought he was going to tell her that he'd promised to cover someone else's shifts and he'd bought the flowers out of guilt.

Well, he *had* bought them out of guilt.

'I thought maybe we could, um, spend some time together, tonight. Talk,' he muttered.

'Oliver, I can't. It's the school PTA committee meeting tonight and I have to be there—I'm the chair. I can't just back out at the last minute and let everyone down.' She sighed. 'It's been booked for weeks. You know I write everything on the calendar.'

The one that hung by the phone. The one he never really took any notice of.

'Why don't you ever look at it?' she asked, almost as if she'd read his thoughts.

Because, if there was anything important, Rachel always reminded him. She hadn't bothered this morning. So it wasn't his fault he'd forgotten, was it? 'Some other time, then. Soon,' he added.

But when? Not tomorrow—that was his trauma medicine course. Thursday was the practice late night. Maybe Friday, then.

When had life become so complicated? When had he and Rachel stopped having time for each other? More to the point, how were they going to fix it? Right now, he didn't have any answers.

On Thursday morning, Rachel was surprised to see Megan Garner halfway through the morning. The practice antenatal clinics were held on Wednesdays, and she'd seen Megan last week. 'Hi, Meg. I thought I was seeing you next Wednesday?'

'You are.' Megan's face was ashen and there were dark shadows under her eyes—more than Rachel expected to see, even though Megan was probably having the usual difficulty sleeping in late pregnancy.

'What's up?'

'It's Jasmine. She's got chickenpox.' A tear trickled down Megan's face. 'I haven't had it. Ever. I played with all the kids in the village and I never, ever got chickenpox. And my mum's friend said chickenpox can—can ki—' She broke off, her breath shuddering, clearly too distraught to say the word, and scrubbed at her eyes with the back of her hand.

'Hey.' Rachel took her hand. 'Of course you're worried. And I'm glad you came to see me. First things first, we don't know you haven't had chickenpox.'

'Mum said I didn't.'

'It's possible that you had it so mildly, you only had one

or two spots and your mum thought they were gnat bites,' Rachel reassured her. 'Studies show that eighty per cent of people who can't recall having chickenpox are actually immune. And chickenpox in pregnancy is really rare—only about three in every thousand pregnant women get it.'

'What about the baby?'

'Yes, there is a risk of the baby developing problems such as skin scarring, eye problems and neurological problems, but that's only a risk if you get it between thirteen and twenty weeks. So you can stop worrying about birth defects because you're well past twenty weeks.' She paused. 'When did Jasmine go down with it?'

'She got the first spots yesterday. She was in the bath and I saw them.' Megan shook her head. 'I'd heard you can literally see chickenpox spots coming out, but I thought people were exaggerating. But I could see them popping up on her back.'

Rachel nodded, calculating mentally that Jasmine became infectious four days ago. The incubation period was between ten days and three weeks, so if Megan did develop chickenpox it would be somewhere between the end of the following week and the next fortnight. 'Right. You're due to have the baby in ten days' time. If the baby's late, that could mean you'll deliver the baby in three weeks' time. Jasmine's spots will all have crusted over by the end of next week, so there shouldn't be any risk to the baby from Jasmine.'

'What about if I have the baby early? Or if I get it?'

'Let's not panic yet. There's a very high probability that you're already immune—remember, around ninety-five per cent of adults have already had it—so I'll do a blood test and ask the lab to rush it through for me. If you're not immune, I can refer you to the hospital for preventative treatment—they can give you something called VZIG and give the baby the same thing when he's born.' She smiled. 'That stands for ''varicella zoster''—chickenpox to me and you—"immunoglobulin". They're antibodies which will protect you and the baby against developing chickenpox.'

Megan was shaking slightly. 'But if I do get it—or the baby?'

'If you get it before you have the baby, we can give you an antiviral medication called acyclovir. We can also give the baby antibodies and the antiviral medication.' Rachel thought it prudent not to mention that ten per cent of pregnant women with chickenpox went on to develop pneumonia—Megan didn't smoke, so that cut her risk anyway—or how serious chickenpox could be for newborns. Until they knew whether Megan was immune or not, Rachel didn't want to panic her patient. 'How's Jasmine?'

'Miserable.'

'If she's got a temperature, you can give her some infant paracetamol or ibuprofen to bring it down.'

'She hasn't said she's hot, just itchy. I keep telling her not to scratch, but she can't help it. Mum says I should put calamine lotion on her.'

'That'll help to stop the itch—though there's something out now that stops the itch for a bit longer and isn't quite as messy.' Rachel scribbled a note on her pad, tore off the top sheet and handed it to Megan. 'You don't need a prescription for this. If Ian at the pharmacy doesn't have it, he can tell you who does stock it or what's the next best thing. Putting a bit of bicarb soda in a tepid bath can help, too. If it's affecting her sleep, bring her to see me and I can give her some antihistamines to stop the itch and help her sleep. She might have a sore throat, so give her plenty of cool drinks. Otherwise, I'd recommend keeping Jasmine's nails really short and doing things with her that keep her hands occupied so she can't scratch. Make sure you get enough rest, though.' She smiled at Megan. 'Do you want a glass of water before I do the scary needle thing?'

Megan shook her head, smiling back. 'No, I'm OK. At least you don't leave bruises. Lucy does.'

'Poor Lucy. She's paranoid that half my mums ask her to let me do the blood samples instead of her.'

'So, has Sophie had chickenpox yet?' Megan asked, looking away as Rachel deftly took the blood sample.

'No. I saw the notice up at nursery this morning. I'll be watching her for the next couple of weeks.' Rachel put her hand flat on the desk. 'Touch wood, we haven't had the nits notice up for a while.'

'Oh, no. Don't talk that up!' Megan groaned.

'Nits scare me a lot more than they scare Soph. She refuses to let me put her hair in a ponytail. And she hates even a detangling comb in her hair—I dread to think what she'd be like with a nit comb,' Rachel said ruefully. 'OK, you can press on the cotton wool for a few seconds.'

'You're done already?'

'I'm done. Not so bad, was it?' Rachel wrote out the lab form. 'I'll ring you as soon as I get the results through. It probably won't be until Monday, but don't spend the weekend fretting about it. There's a very, very strong chance that you're immune—and if you're not, we can protect you and the baby.'

'Thanks, Rachel.' Megan took a deep breath. 'I feel a bit better now.'

'Good. If you're worried, talk to me or Lucy, OK? That's what we're here for.' The calmer Megan stayed, the better her blood pressure would be—and the better it would be for the baby.

When Rachel had finished surgery, she checked with Rita that Oliver didn't have a patient with him, then knocked on Oliver's door. At his 'Come in' she put her head round the door.

'Good or bad time?' she asked.

He pulled a face. 'Not brilliant.'

'OK, then, I'll keep it short. Chickenpox is doing the rounds again. The note's up on the nursery door. If Soph gets it, we're going to need locum cover for one of us where our shifts overlap.' It would probably be her, but she'd give Oliver the option of nursing their daughter if he wanted to.

Oliver rolled his eyes. 'That's all I need. Good locums are—'

'Like gold dust,' Rachel finished. She'd heard him say it so often. 'That's why you're getting advance warning. So you can be prepared. I'm not saying Soph's definitely going to get it.'

'But it's one of the most infectious viruses, it spreads by droplets in the air, and ninety per cent of susceptible contacts get it.' Oliver sighed. 'I hope she doesn't get it as badly as Rob did.'

'Me, too.' Rachel paused. 'Um, it's Sophie's full day at nursery today. Want to meet me for lunch in the Red Lion for one of their bacon and Brie baguettes?' If that didn't tempt him, nothing would.

'Sorry, I can't. I've got a pile of house calls, plus I'm seeing a drug rep, and I've already put him off four times.'

'Right.' So it was nothing, then. She shrugged. 'Just thought I'd ask.'

'Rach—'

'Doesn't matter.' She wanted to get away before the tears pricking at the back of her eyelids got any worse. Stupid, feeling rejected by her own husband. He was *busy*. She knew that. But all the same she wished he'd just grab a little bit of time to spend with her. She forced a smile to her face. 'See you at home.'

'Don't forget, it's late surgery tonight for me,' he reminded her.

As if she could forget. Oliver spent more time at the practice than he did at home nowadays. 'Sure,' she said, hoping that he didn't hear the wobble in her voice, and left his consulting room.

When Oliver came home after evening surgery, he handed Rachel a box wrapped in gold paper and a matching ribbon. 'For you,' he said with a smile.

Belgian chocolates. Her absolute favourites. She knew she ought to throw her arms around him and say thank you, but something stopped her. *Why* was he buying her chocolates? It wasn't the sort of thing that Oliver did.

Unbidden, the words from the magazine article floated back into her mind. *Your partner buys you lots of gifts because he feels guilty about betraying you and showering you with presents makes him feel better.* Before she could stop herself, the words were out. 'Flowers on Tuesday, chocolates tonight... Is there something I should be worried about?'

Oliver bridled. 'Look, I just felt guilty that I couldn't have lunch with you when you asked me. For God's sake, I thought you'd like them. But I can't do anything right where you're concerned.' He scowled. 'Maybe you ought to start taking evening primrose oil.'

'What?' She stared at him. What was he driving at?

'It's meant to help mood swings.'

He thought she was having PMT? Or, even worse, early menopause? For goodness' sake, she was only thirty-four! She shook her head. 'Oliver, I'm not having mood swings.'

'Look, I understand about PMT. I'm a modern man, not a dinosaur.'

'Yeah, right.'

He frowned. 'What's that supposed to mean?'

'Just leave it. I'm going to have a bath. There's ham and salad in the fridge, and French bread in the bread bin. If you want dinner, you can get it yourself.'

'Rach—'

'Leave it,' she said again, and walked quickly away. Oh, God. This was unbearable. If Oliver really was having an affair... She shivered. And if he wasn't, and she accused him of having an affair, it would deepen the gulf between them.

How was she going to bridge that gulf? Because if she didn't, there was a good chance her marriage would be over by the end of the summer. They couldn't go on like this.

Oliver didn't come in to talk to her while she was in the bath, and she didn't bother taking a mug of coffee into his office—what was the point, when he'd only snap at her for interrupting? She tried and failed to read the latest thriller from a writer who usually gripped her. All she could think about was Oliver, and how her marriage was crumbling before her eyes and she didn't know how to stop it.

When she heard Oliver coming upstairs, she considered talking to him—but panicked and pretended to be asleep. She noted with an inward sigh that he didn't cuddle into her, turning his back on her instead. Worse, judging by his deep and regular breathing, he fell asleep quickly, whereas she stayed awake until the small hours, trying to work out whether she was just being silly or whether she really *did* have something to worry about.

When Rachel woke the next morning, her eyes felt gritty and her head felt as if someone had whacked it with a sledgehammer. A cool shower and a hairwash helped, and a couple of paracetamol helped even more.

Robin was already getting himself dressed, so Rachel went to wake Sophie. And stopped dead. There were half a dozen spots on the little girl's face. Gently, Rachel pulled the duvet back, lifted Sophie's pyjama top, and saw that Sophie's torso was covered in spots.

Very recognisable spots, red with a blister in the centre. Chickenpox.

She sighed. 'No nursery for you this morning,' she said softly to the sleeping child. 'I'd better ring them and tell them you won't be in until all the spots have crusted over. Which probably won't be for another week.' She stroked her daughter's hair. Best to let her sleep while she could—as soon as Sophie was awake, she'd start to itch and scratch her spots.

Rachel walked back to her bedroom. Oliver sat up, rubbing his eyes, then stretched. 'Is it morning already?'

Oliver never wore a pyjama top. The sight of her husband's muscular shoulders and bare chest sent a shiver of desire through Rachel. But now wasn't the time. 'Bad news. Soph's covered in spots. I'll ask Ginny if she'll take Rob to school with Jack, and I'm afraid you'll have to get a locum in for me or share my list around today.'

Oliver groaned. 'You talked it up yesterday.'

'No. I just warned you it was on the cards. And that meant any time in the next twenty-one days. She can't go back to nursery until the last spots have crusted over, so I won't be working for the next week—unless you'd rather stay home with Sophie?'

Sophie would adore having her daddy all to herself. And Oliver would learn all about Pwintheth Mouse—maybe nursing his daughter through her illness was the wake-up call he needed. The thing that would make him start concentrating on his family.

Though Rachel already knew what his reaction was going to be.

'No, she needs her mum with her.'

Sophie needed her dad, too. So did Robin. But Rachel wasn't feeling up to a row. 'If you think it's best,' she said coolly.

He raked a hand through his dark hair. 'Don't worry. I'll sort things out at the practice.' Almost as a second thought, he added, 'Do you need me to bring anything home for Sophie?'

'Antipruritic lotion. The itching's going to drive her crackers, and I can't make her sit in the bath all day. I don't really want to take her out until her spots have crusted over, though.'

'Sure.' Oliver climbed out of bed and headed for their shower room.

Hell. Why did he have to look so *sexy* when she didn't have time to do anything about it? Since they'd had the children, they didn't spend Sunday mornings in bed any more. Rachel realised just how much she missed it, the warmth of her husband's body heating hers, tangled limbs, the roughness of the hairs on his chest against her skin.

Then she remembered last night. The guilt-gift—chocolates that she hadn't been able to face eating, because she knew why he'd bought them and they would have stuck in her throat.

Ha. What was the point of lusting after a man who'd not only fallen out of lust with you, but had fallen in lust with someone else?

She shook herself, and went to make a start on the calls to rearrange the children's usual routine.

Distracting a small child from scratching the itchy spots was, well, almost impossible, Rachel thought. She'd tried reading the little girl's favourite stories, letting Sophie loose with the CD-ROMs on Oliver's old computer which they kept under the stairs for the kids to use, drawing pictures with her, reading more stories, doing jigsaw puzzles, reading more stories… And now Rachel was more shattered than if she'd gone in to the surgery. The house was a mess—she hadn't even had time to hang the washing out, let alone tidy up—and Sophie was decidedly grumpy.

'Daddy's home!' Sophie yelled.

Since when was delirium a symptom of chickenpox? Rachel wondered. The usual complications were bacterial infection of the spots if they were scratched, ear infections, conjunctivitis and rarely meningitis or encephalitis—inflammation of the brain, which started about four days after the rash first appeared. Any signs of drowsiness, breathing problems, convulsions or a stiff neck and dislike of bright lights and Rachel would drive Sophie straight to the nearest emergency department.

'Daddy, Daddy, Daddy!'

'How's my best girl?' Oliver's deep voice asked.

Rachel blinked and glanced at the clock. Lunchtime. Oliver *never* came home at lunchtime. Ever.

He walked into the kitchen, with Sophie sitting on his shoulders. 'Hi,' he said, giving Rachel the broad grin which had made her fall head over heels for him as a student.

Despite the fear gnawing in her stomach—the fear that today was the day when Oliver would bring everything into the open and she'd learn something she really, really didn't want to know—she couldn't help smiling back. 'This is a nice surprise.'

'I can't stay long—but I thought you'd be going stir-crazy, being cooped up at home, so if you want to go out and have a walk or something?'

Her fairy godmother had definitely been at work. 'Thanks. I could do with ten minutes to myself,' she admitted. 'Want me to make you a sandwich first?'

'No need.' Gently, he lifted Sophie from his shoulders and set her on the floor. 'I brought supplies. Bacon and Brie baguettes to go, from the Red Lion. Plus the stuff to stop the itching. And something special for my little girl.' He fetched a carrier bag from the hall, and fished out five comics for preschoolers.

'Ooh, Daddy! Thank you!' Sophie squeaked.

'And for Robin.' He put a puzzle magazine on the table,

and Rachel blinked in surprise. Oliver had *noticed* that Rob liked doing puzzles?

'And...' He brought out a bottle of red wine and a DVD. A romantic comedy—the sort of film he absolutely hated and Rachel adored. 'Something for us, tonight.'

For *us*? He was actually planning to spend time with her tonight? Rachel was so shocked that she burst into tears.

Immediately, Oliver put his arms round her and held her close. 'Hey. It's OK,' he said, stroking her hair. 'Soph's going to be absolutely fine. Don't worry about work—the practice will manage without you for today, and I've got a locum to cover you from Monday. I've known Caroline Prentiss for years.'

'Caroline Prentiss?' The name sounded familiar, but Rachel couldn't think why.

'She's just moved back into the area—she was looking for a locum job, so that's all sorted. And I've asked Prunella to chase the lab for Megan's serum results.'

Which meant they'd get the results double-quick—everyone was scared of Prunella, except Oliver. 'Thank you,' Rachel muttered against his chest. 'Sorry. I'm just being...' Her voice tailed off.

'You've been cooped up with a sick toddler all morning, and I don't pull my weight in the house. It's no wonder you're feeling tired and tearful.'

And relieved, Rachel thought. This was the Oliver she knew and loved: a workaholic, but one who still found time for those he loved. Maybe he was right. Maybe they'd just been at cross-purposes these last few months. Everything was going to be all right.

'Why's Mummy crying?' Sophie wanted to know.

'Because she's feeling a bit out of sorts, too,' Oliver said. He kissed the top of Rachel's head, then stepped back. 'Right, you. Go and get some fresh air for five minutes. I'll make us a coffee, then we'll have lunch together. Just like we should have done yesterday.'

When he'd been too busy. And he was even busier today, covering for her as well as doing his own list. Guilt flooded through her. 'You had to cancel things, didn't you?'

He shrugged. 'They can wait.' He smiled. 'Five minutes. Or I'll eat your baguette as well as my own!'

She knew that look. Teasing, loving… Her husband was back. And he wasn't—absolutely *wasn't*—having an affair. He loved her, she loved him, and all was right with her world again.

So why was there still that little niggle in the back of her mind?

# CHAPTER FOUR

OLIVER worked that evening, just as Rachel knew he would. But when she was reading a story to Sophie, he came upstairs to kiss the children goodnight. Then he took her hand and led her downstairs into the living room. It wasn't dark outside but he'd already pulled the curtains.

'Just you and me now,' he whispered. 'You, me, a film and a bottle of wine.'

He'd uncorked the Merlot to let it breathe; he poured two glasses and handed one to her. 'It's been too long since we did this, Rach.'

And whose fault is that? she wanted to ask. Who is it who spends every minute in his wretched office in the evenings? But she took a sip of wine instead, savouring the taste.

He took the glass from her hand, set it down beside his own, then sprawled on the sofa and patted the space next to him. 'Come here.'

She lay with her back to him, spoon-style, and his arm curved round her, pulling her back against him. It was how they'd often spent Friday nights when Robin had been tiny, watching a good film together and sharing a bottle of wine. They'd have the baby listener turned down low—the flashing lights would tell them if Robin was crying—and often they'd only catch the first half of the film, because then Oliver would start to kiss the back of her neck and slide his hand under the hem of her top, and they'd be so lost in exploring each other that the film would be forgotten.

Did he remember those nights, too? Maybe, because the arm around her waist tightened. Rachel relaxed against him.

It felt so good to be in Oliver's arms again, to feel the warmth of his body against hers.

'Rach,' he whispered, nuzzling her shoulder and she arched back against him. He kissed along the line of her neck. 'I love the way you smell,' he murmured. 'The way you taste.' His hand slipped under the hem of her top and he cupped her breast. 'The way you feel.'

Which was exactly the way she felt about him. She twisted round so she was facing him, and cupped his face in her hands. 'Me, too,' she whispered, and kissed him.

'I want you so much,' he told her when he broke the kiss. His pupils were huge, edged with a narrow rim of blue, so his eyes looked almost black with passion.

Everything was going to be all right. They were going to make love, and everything was going to be all right.

Slowly, he undid the button of her jeans and slid the zip down. He teased her, his fingers drifting over her midriff; Rachel made a small sound of impatience and tilted her hips.

'Something you wanted, Dr Bedingfield?' he asked, his voice low and husky.

'You,' she replied, her voice equally husky.

'I think that can be arranged.' He gave her a smile that managed to be teasing yet smouldering at the same time, and a thrill of desire ran down her spine.

It didn't take him long to remove her jeans—or her to remove his. Her top followed, then his T-shirt. And finally they were skin to skin. Rachel could still remember the first time they'd made love in her narrow single bed at university, the heady excitement of exploring each other's body fully for the first time, learning where each other liked to be touched and stroked and kissed. That headiness had never quite gone away, for her. Even now, she thrilled at how good Oliver's body felt against her own.

And right now he was all hers.

'Rachel.' He breathed her name as he kissed his way

down her collar-bone, stroked the length of her spine, then finally took the hard peak of one nipple into his mouth.

Rachel couldn't help closing her eyes, concentrating on the sensations evoked by his clever mouth. All she could feel was Oliver, all she could sense, all she could—

'Mum-*mee*!'

They both stilled.

'Maybe she'll go back to sleep,' Oliver mumbled against Rachel's skin.

As if to contradict him, Sophie's wail grew louder. 'Mum-*mee*!' she sobbed again.

If Rachel could have cloned herself at that moment, she'd have been happy. As it was, whatever she did she lost. Sophie was ill and needed her—Rachel couldn't possibly desert her sick child. But Oliver... This was the first time in weeks they'd been close. Who knew when her husband would let her get this close again?

Damned if I stay, damned if I go, Rachel thought, her heart feeling as if it had been torn in half. She pulled away from Oliver regretfully, and slipped her jeans and T-shirt back on. 'I'd better go to her. She's not well. If we leave her, she'll get into a state and it'll take us for ever to calm her down again.'

'Sure.'

'Can you bring a drink up for her and the infant paracetamol?' And maybe if Oliver stayed with her, maybe if they cared for their daughter together—then maybe when Sophie fell asleep again they could take up where they'd left off.

Though she knew she was kidding herself: he was already reaching for his own clothes. It didn't take a genius to know what he'd be doing while she was settling Sophie again.

Oliver brought up a spill-proof beaker of water, so it wouldn't matter if their daughter went to sleep still holding her cup—she wouldn't get drenched and wake up again. He poured the infant paracetamol into a spoon for Sophie and encouraged her to take it. And then he uttered the words Rachel had been expecting and dreading in equal measure: 'I'll just do a bit of admin while you're here with Sophie.'

If only you'd slept just a few minutes longer, Rachel thought, rocking her daughter to sleep in her arms. If your father and I had made love, everything would have been all right. Now, who knows? Work will come between us yet again.

When Sophie had drifted back to sleep, and Rachel padded barefoot into Oliver's office holding a glass of Merlot, her husband didn't even look up. 'You go ahead and watch the film. I'll be in with you in a minute.'

His definition of 'in a minute' definitely wasn't the same as his wife's, because he was still working when the film had finished. And Rachel's mood had cooled to the point where she didn't want to make love any more—what was the point, when she clearly came so far down Oliver's list of priorities?

He didn't reach for her in bed that night either. Which in some ways was just as well, because Sophie woke several times, each time feeling itchy and out of sorts and wanting comfort from her mother. Rachel felt like a zombie from lack of sleep the next morning, and her mood hadn't improved by Saturday evening, when Oliver appeared, freshly showered, wearing smart black trousers and a casual silk shirt.

'Aren't you getting changed?' Oliver asked.

She stared at him. Changed? 'Why?'

'My mother's drinks party. We're supposed to be going, remember?'

Rachel shook her head. 'I told you this morning, I rang her and explained that Sophie was ill and I can't leave her.' Surely he wasn't going to suggest that they should still ask Ginny to babysit, when Sophie was ill and miserable and wanting her parents? She bit back her irritation. 'You can still go, if you want.' On his own. Leaving her to do all the nursing.

'I promised her we'd be there.' Oliver emphasised the 'we'. 'She called me to remind me this afternoon.'

Doing his usual power-play thing: making his son choose between his old family and his new one. Even after all these years Isabel hadn't quite forgiven Rachel for Oliver doing something against his family's wishes—as if Oliver wasn't a grown man, perfectly able to make his own decisions. 'Look, Sophie's ill and she wants me with her. Your mother understands that a babysitter—even someone Sophie knows really well, like Ginny—just isn't an option.' Though Isabel had made it very clear she considered it a feeble excuse on Rachel's part. No doubt that was why she'd phoned Oliver, expecting him to pressure Rachel into going. Stupid, really, when Rachel didn't even fit in with the Bedingfields' social set. She still had the wrong accent, even though her Geordie accent had softened over the years.

Hell. She was sleep-deprived and she really didn't feel like facing the Bedingfields tonight. The barbs she usually managed to ignore would go deep. Why couldn't Isabel just have accepted the situation? Why had she had to put that extra little bit of pressure on Oliver—pressure neither of them needed right now?

'My mother's relying on us to help,' Oliver said, his mouth thinning.

No. More like Nigel's come up with one of his flimsy excuses for not being there, and she wants to boast about *one* of her sons, Rachel thought grimly. The one who can be relied on. The one she takes for granted. The one who's still good-natured enough to run around after her and not mind when she drops him like a hot potato the second that her precious Nigel makes an appearance. 'Sorry. Sophie comes first.'

Oliver's eyes narrowed, as if he suspected she was being

critical about him. Oh, for goodness' sake! It wasn't *about* him and his bloody family. It was about the fact that their daughter was ill and wanted at least one parent at home with her. 'And I could do with an early night, to catch up on the sleep I missed last night.' When she, not Oliver, had comforted their daughter.

'Of course.' A muscle flickered in his jaw.

'Go and have a nice time,' Rachel said, giving him a placating smile. Bloody Isabel. She must have some kind of sixth sense, to know just when things weren't going that well between Oliver and Rachel and just where to bring the extra pressure to bear. Sometimes Rachel thought that Isabel would prefer the stigma—in Isabel's eyes, at least—of having a divorced son to having a daughter-in-law with the wrong accent.

'Right. Well, I'll have to stay until the end—I can't leave my mother to clear up everything on her own.'

Meaning he thought that Rachel would? That was unfair. Anyway, Isabel always employed waitresses to deal with guests at drinks parties. Isabel did all the meeting and greeting, gracefully working the room with a champagne cocktail in one hand and a tinkly little laugh. Refilling glasses and plates and clearing away were left to her minions. And to suckers like Rachel who'd been brought up to muck in and do her share of the dirty work. 'Then I'll see you tomorrow morning.'

Oliver's goodbye kiss was distinctly cool—more like a peck than a proper kiss. Rachel pulled a face at the door as she heard his car pull away, then made a bowl of popcorn in the microwave and let the children stay up to watch a film. Sophie fell asleep on Rachel's lap, and Rachel had just shepherded Robin to bed and tucked Sophie in when the doorbell rang.

Not Oliver, surely. He had his keys—besides, she didn't think he'd be back early. Once Isabel had her prize, she wouldn't let him go until the very last second. Unless Nigel turned up, in which case Isabel would barely even glance in Oliver's direction. The sad thing was, Oliver was so used to it that it didn't even bother him. Though it annoyed the hell out of Rachel. Her own parents treated Rachel and her sister equally: why couldn't the Bedingfields do the same?

Frowning, Rachel answered the door.

'Much-needed supplies,' Ginny said, waving a box of chocolates at her. 'Now, remembering how I felt when Jack had chickenpox, either you're sleep-deprived or you're stir-crazy.'

'Probably a bit of both,' Rachel admitted with a wry smile. 'Thanks, Ginny. Want a glass of wine?'

'Love one.' Ginny followed her into the kitchen and accepted a glass of chilled pinot grigio. 'So how's Soph?'

'Itchy and grumpy,' Rachel said, rolling her eyes. 'Still, at least Oliver's managed to find me a locum—Caroline Prentiss.'

'*She's* back, then.'

Something in Ginny's tone sent a shiver through Rachel. 'What do you mean by that, Ginny?'

'Um—never mind.' Ginny's smile was clearly fake. 'Just ignore me.'

Rachel frowned. 'Ginny, you're my friend, right?'

'Of course I am.'

'So tell me what you meant. Please.'

Ginny sighed. 'Caroline used to go out with Oliver. Way, way before he met you—but I think everyone expected them to get married. Anyway, they broke up and then he met you.'

Ice washed over Rachel. Why had Oliver never mentioned Caroline to her before? Neither had Isabel, which Rachel found strange. Surely Caroline would be the yard-stick Rachel was measured against and failed? Or was Caroline the reason why Isabel had disapproved of Rachel so much in the early days, viewing her as a relationship-breaker? But when he'd asked her out, Oliver had told her he was single. He wouldn't have lied to her. So maybe Caroline was on Isabel's blacklist, too, as the woman who broke Oliver's heart. 'So he was on the rebound, then?'

As soon as the words were out, Rachel wished them unsaid. She didn't want anyone thinking that Oliver had kept her in the dark about Caroline—even though he had.

'I didn't say that. Don't be silly.' Ginny shook her head. 'Oliver adores you and the kids. Everyone can see that.'

Rachel, thinking of that magazine article again, wasn't so sure.

Ginny sighed again. 'Look, don't worry about it. I know he works stupid hours, but that's because of his family. If Nigel wasn't such a worthless toad, Oliver wouldn't feel he had to make up for him as well.'

Rachel smiled wryly. 'How well you know my in-laws.'

'I grew up around here, remember? Oliver's a couple of years older than me and he went to a different school, but everyone knew the Bedingfields. Anyway, look on the bright side. Soph might be ill and grumpy and you might feel like a zombie, but at least you've escaped Lady Bedingfield's drinks party tonight.'

Oliver's parents weren't titled, but Isabel Bedingfield always acted as if she were lady of the manor, and the village nickname had stuck. Rachel wasn't so sure that it was an affectionate nickname either; her mother-in-law was known for being finicky and expecting people to jump to attention whenever she snapped her fingers.

'So what's Caroline like?' she asked.

Ginny shrugged. 'I haven't seen her for years. She was in Oliver's year so she left school before I did, and once she escaped Hollybridge she hardly ever came back. She used to be tall, thin and pretty, with blonde hair down to her waist—the type who'd manage to look glamorous in a bin bag,' she added with a wry smile. 'But you couldn't hate her for it because she was nice with it. She was the one everyone wanted to *be* in our school.'

'And Isabel approved of her, I suppose?' The words were out before Rachel could stop them.

'Well, yes. She's the vicar's daughter.'

Of *course*. That was why she'd half recognised the name. Now Rachel thought about it, she remembered that the Prentisses were friendly with the Bedingfields. But she couldn't remember anyone called Caroline coming to their wedding. As a friend of the family, why hadn't Caroline been invited to the wedding?

Or hadn't it really been all over between Oliver and Caroline? No way could Rachel have watched the man she loved marrying someone else. Maybe it had been the same for Caroline. Isabel had insisted on handling the invitations, so maybe Caroline had been invited and had declined.

Ginny looked at her, frowning slightly. 'Rachel, is everything OK?'

'Yes, of course.' If you discounted the fact that her husband's gorgeous ex-girlfriend—one who was actually accepted by the Bedingfields, by the sound of it—was back on the scene. Would she expect to return to Oliver's private life as well as his working life?

Rachel gave herself a mental kick. Now she was just being paranoid. And there was no point in speculating about the reasons why Oliver and Caroline had split up in the first place. It was in the past, it had been over years and years ago, and he was married with a family. 'Let's start on the chocolates before Soph wakes up in a grump,' she said.

'Sounds good to me,' Ginny said with a grin.

When Ginny had gone, Rachel put a film on, but she couldn't concentrate. Oliver and Caroline. Their names even sounded right together.

Why hadn't Oliver ever said anything to her about Caroline? Especially now she was Rachel's locum. He really should have put her in the picture, told her more than just 'I've known her for years'. Or was he deliberately keeping her in the dark?

'Snap out of it,' she told herself loudly. 'You can ask him when he gets home. Get some sleep first.'

But she couldn't sleep. She wasn't distracted by music, a book, a crossword. Sophie woke twice and needed comforting, but that left way too many minutes for Rachel to fill on her own. Too many minutes for her to wonder about Caroline Prentiss.

It was nearly one in the morning when Oliver came in.

'I thought you'd be asleep,' he said, when he came into their bedroom and discovered Rachel reading.

She put the book down. 'It's too hot.' Remember, no accusations, she reminded herself. Don't start a row. Be tactful. 'Did you have a nice time?'

'The usual.'

'Anyone interesting there?'

He frowned. 'What is this, twenty questions?'

'Just showing an interest.' She shrugged. 'If I hadn't asked, you'd think I was being sniffy. I can't win, can I?'

'Sorry.' He raked one hand through his hair.

Did he look guilty, or was that her imagination? And how could she tactfully raise the subject of Caroline?

'I meant to ask you yesterday—how's my locum getting on?'

'Caroline? Fine.'

Ask a closed question, get a one-word answer. She should know better than that.

'You said you'd known her for years. Did she grow up round here, then?'

'She's the vicar's daughter.'

So he wasn't going to admit that Caroline was also his

ex. 'Oh, right. I don't remember her being at our wedding reception.'

'She wasn't.'

Because she hadn't been invited—because Oliver couldn't get over the fact she'd broken his heart? Or because she hadn't been able to face the love of her life marrying someone else? Rachel could hardly ask, and Oliver definitely wasn't telling. There was no way she could ask whether Caroline had been there tonight either, without Oliver wanting to know why she was asking—and discovering that she'd been talking to Ginny about Caroline. And then he'd be irritated that she'd been discussing their marriage with someone else. Oliver had always been a very, very private person.

Which just left Rachel a seething mass of questions. What a mess.

'Right. Well, see you in the morning,' she said, closing her book and settling back against the pillow.

'I'll have a shower before I come to bed. I reek of smoke,' he said.

Isabel didn't allow people to smoke in her house, so Oliver couldn't possibly have reeked of smoke. Though Rachel didn't think anything of it until the following afternoon, when Oliver had been called out to a patient who'd had an accident and his mobile phone beeped.

He'd be cross that he'd left his phone behind. And maybe it had been a patient: she really ought to check. But there was nothing on the 'missed call' screen.

Then she saw the little envelope on the screen. She hadn't heard a call—she'd heard a text arriving.

Something made her flip into the 'read messages' screen. Though she didn't open the message. She just stared at the readout. 'C'. Who was 'C'? Frowning, she scrolled through Oliver's phone list. As she'd expected, 'C' was there, but it wasn't a number she recognised. They had no friends, family or colleagues whose first name or surname started with C.

Except Caroline Prentiss.

Why would Caroline be texting Oliver? And, if it was so innocent, why hadn't he listed her under her full name, as he did everyone else—why just her initial? Nausea rose in her stomach. Maybe Oliver hadn't been washing off the scent of smoke last might. Maybe he'd been washing off the scent of Caroline Prentiss.

Knowing she shouldn't do it, Rachel pressed 'Read'. And stared at the message on the screen.

*Have you told her yet? C x*

# CHAPTER FIVE

TOLD her what? That he was seeing Caroline, having an affair? That he was going to leave her?

'Oh—my—God,' Rachel said softly.

So the magazine article had been right after all. Oliver was having an affair. With his ex.

Her whole body was shaking. This was the last thing she'd ever, ever expected from Oliver. He was a good man, and family meant a lot to him—look at the way he'd changed his own career plans to be an accident and emergency specialist and become a GP so he could step in and take over from his father at the practice. He wouldn't have an affair. He just *wouldn't*.

But the message was very clear.

*Have you told her yet?*

It had guilt written all over it.

What the hell was she going to do?

Still shaking, she went to look in on the children, who were building Lego structures in Robin's bedroom. Surely Oliver wasn't going to leave the children. And then a really nasty thought hit her. Supposing he expected *her* to leave and the children to stay with him?

No way. Absolutely *no way*. She wasn't giving up her children for anyone. If Caroline thought it was going to be easy to step into her shoes, Caroline would be in for a shock—because she'd fight to the death before she would let her children be taken away from her.

'Mummy, your face is a funny colour,' Robin said. 'Are you getting chickenpox, too?'

'No, darling. I'm just tired.' And shocked. But Robin was

only six. He didn't need to know about the complications of adult life. Or that his father was a lying, cheating louse. She forced her voice to sound normal. 'Do you want a drink?'

'*I* want a drink!' Sophie added, her baby voice imperious.

'Word missing,' Rachel corrected automatically.

'Please,' Sophie lisped.

'Me, too. Please,' Robin added hastily.

'I'll bring something up to you,' Rachel promised, and went downstairs. She replaced the mobile phone where Oliver had left it, took the children their drinks, then sat at the bottom of the stairs with the cordless phone. She needed to talk to someone about this. Someone close—and someone sensible, who'd tell her if she was blowing this out of proportion and misreading everything.

The phone seemed to ring for ever. Rachel was on the point of hanging up when her elder sister answered the phone.

'Oh, Fi.' She almost sagged in relief. 'It's Rach. Is this a good time?'

'Not really—hang on, Rach, are you OK?' Concern radiated down the line.

'Not really,' Rachel said, her voice wobbling.

'OK. I'm just going to put a film on for the kids to distract them—just keep talking,' her elder sister directed. 'Even if I sound as if I'm not paying attention, I am, OK? What's happened?'

'Oliver,' Rachel whispered.

'Is he ill? Been in an accident?'

'Nothing like that.' He was at an accident, yes, but as the medical help, not as the victim. 'Fi, have you ever wondered if Mark was having an affair?'

'No.' Rachel could almost hear the frown in her sister's voice. 'Rach, surely you're not saying *Oliver's* having an affair?'

'I think so.'

'No way. Rach, he adores you. He's fought for you, too—look how he stood up against his parents when they tried to split you up.'

Rachel swallowed. 'That's just the point.' She filled Fiona in on her suspicions.

'Oh.' Fiona exhaled sharply. 'Rach, I can't believe it. He—well, he's just not the *type*.'

And Fiona would know: as a specialist in family law, she'd seen enough divorce cases. 'I didn't think so either. But what else could it be?'

'Look, you must have got the wrong end of the stick. Just talk to him about it.'

'I dunno, Fi. If I'm wrong, he's—he's never going to forgive me for not trusting him. And if I'm right... I'm scared. Supposing he wants a divorce? Supposing he wants to be with her, and take the kids, and...?' She broke off on a sob.

'Rach, stop panicking. You're not going to lose the kids. If it comes to a divorce, you'll have the very best legal team on your side, I promise you that. I'm not allowed to handle it, but I can oversee the team and make damned sure your kids stay with you.'

Rachel gulped. 'Thanks, Fi. I never thought I'd...that I'd be a statistic.'

'You're not, yet.' Fiona sighed. 'Bottom line. Do you still love him?'

'Yes.'

'And would you take him back, even if he's been unfaithful? Remember, you don't have any definite proof yet, just a suspicion.'

'Yes.' Life without Oliver was unthinkable. She'd fallen in love with him years ago—virtually the first time she'd met him. Oliver and the kids were her whole world.

'Then you've got two options. Confront him and ask

what's going on, then deal with the consequences. Or don't say anything and fight for your man. Win him back.'

'Supposing he doesn't want to come back?'

'Course he will. Look, you're just going through a bad patch. You're both working, you've got two small kids, and there aren't enough hours in the day to fit everything in. You're both probably feeling neglected and taken for granted, and things are a bit rough right now. Every marriage goes through patches like that. But you've been together for—what, twelve years?'

'Fourteen,' Rachel admitted.

'That's a lot of time, a lot of emotional investment. He's not going to throw that away on a whim.'

'How come you know so much?'

Fiona chuckled. 'I'll ask you the same next time one of my kids is ill and I'm panicking and you're calming me down and explaining that a headache doesn't mean it's meningitis.'

'Years of training and experience, seeing it in other people,' Rachel said wryly.

'Exactly. Talking of kids, how are my favourite niece and nephew?'

'Rob's fine and Soph's got chickenpox.'

'And you're doing all the nursing?' Fiona guessed.

'Oliver's busy at work.'

'So you're sleep-deprived as well.' Fiona coughed. 'I think you're blowing things out of proportion, love. There's probably a good reason for this text message—something innocent. Oliver loves you to bits. Why else would he have married you, instead of some nice girl with the right accent to suit his bloody mother?'

'Maybe the guilt's just worn off,' Rachel said. 'Maybe he's had time to regret it. Marry in haste, repent at leisure.'

'You didn't get married in haste. You lived together first.'

'Mmm.' And that had got right up Isabel's nose: the idea

of her precious son cohabiting. Socially, that was even worse in her eyes than being married to someone with the wrong accent.

'I think you and Oliver just need some couple time. A second honeymoon, even if it's only for a couple of days. Look, I can't get any time off for a fortnight or so, because I can't shift my case-load, but if you want me to have the kids for a couple of days in the school holidays that's fine— I'll come down and pick them up even.'

'Thanks, Fi. I might take you up on that.'

'No "might" about it. Do it. Oh.' Fiona growled. 'Sometimes I wish I didn't live up here in Newcastle! If I'd stayed in London, I could have been with you within an hour. Look, I'll get the next train down. It's three and a half hours from here to London, then if I change at King's Cross for Victoria, I should be with you in—'

'Fi, it's OK. Really. I'm fine,' Rachel lied. Right then, she would have given a great deal to see her elder sister. But she couldn't expect Fiona to spend the best part of five hours on a train—with lots of hanging about in between, as it was Sunday service—and get back again the same night ready for work in the morning. Fi was right. There just weren't enough hours in the day.

'Right now, it sounds like you need a hug.'

'You're talking to me. That's enough.' Rachel's voice wobbled.

'Rach, everything's going to be fine. I promise. You're tired, you and Oliver are going through a bad patch, and you just need some time for the two of you.'

'But what if he *is* having an affair?'

'Then you need to think about what you want. If you want out, you need evidence for a fault divorce. If you want him to stay, then you have to fight for him. Win him back. Though that means forgiving him—*really* forgiving him. If you don't trust him, it'll corrode your relationship and eventually you'll start to hate him,' Fiona warned.

'I just want things to be as they were. Me, Oliver and the kids. We were happy.' Rachel drew a deep breath. 'Sometimes I wish we'd never come to Hollybridge. If Oliver had done what he wanted to do, become an emergency medicine specialist, and I'd been a paediatric specialist—if we'd stayed in London or even moved back home—then we wouldn't be right under his mother's nose the whole time.'

'He might have hated it here in Newcastle,' Fiona pointed out gently.

'I suppose so.'

'And you're not under Isabel's nose. She lives on the other side of the village.'

And hardly ever came to see the grandchildren. Rachel or Oliver always had to take the kids over to see Isabel. If Rachel's parents had lived that close, they'd have been far more hands-on. They'd have offered to babysit, taken some of the strain off. Rachel envied her friends whose parents lived nearby and delighted in their grandchildren. Isabel—on the two occasions when Rachel had asked her to babysit—had made it very clear it was an enormous favour and had put her out severely. And yet at the same time Isabel seemed to oversee absolutely everything and made judgements—usually disapproving. It drove Rachel bananas, but she tried to hold her tongue. At the end of the day, Isabel was still Oliver's mother and, despite the way she treated him, Oliver loved her. Speaking her mind would achieve nothing but ill feeling. She'd already learned that the hard way.

Right at that moment Rachel felt like bundling the children into the car and spending the rest of the day driving up to Newcastle. She wanted her family round her: people who accepted her for who she was. Who *loved* her for who she was. But eight hours of motorway driving wouldn't be much fun for the kids; and Sophie was ill; and it wasn't fair to take Rob out of school just because she was feeling miserable; and then there was the nagging feeling that if she left Oliver, even for a couple of days, it would be tantamount to admitting defeat and letting Caroline win.

'Go and make yourself a cup of tea. *Proper* tea, strong enough to stand the spoon up in, with three sugars for shock,' Fiona counselled. 'Then, when Oliver gets back, talk to him about getting some time together. A second honeymoon. I'll have the kids. Or you can ask Mum.' She laughed. 'On second thoughts, better stick to me. Mum'll spoil them rotten and Soph will be a monster when you get her back.'

Rachel smiled unwillingly. 'And you wouldn't spoil them rotten?'

'Auntie's privilege,' Fiona informed her.

'Thanks for listening, Fi.'

'No probs. That's what family's for.'

Her family, anyway. Oliver's were the least supportive bunch Rachel had ever met. Or maybe it was because they still hadn't forgiven Oliver for making a stand against them and marrying the girl with the wrong accent. He jumped through hoops for them, even ran the practice the same way that his father had, and still it wasn't good enough for them. Whereas Nigel could be as selfish and thoughtless as he wanted to be, and Isabel didn't seem to notice. In fact, she deliberately turned a blind eye and made up the most flimsy excuses for him. Excuses that Oliver would never, ever have been allowed to get away with.

Why couldn't Isabel be *fair* about things?

Rachel swallowed back the threatening tears. 'I'll ring you later, Fi.'

'Any time. Even if it's three in the morning. You know I'm here for you. *Nihil te bastardes carborundorum*, OK?'

Dog Latin: don't let the bastards grind you down. Rachel smiled. 'I won't. Take care, Fi.'

'You, too, sis.'

When Rachel cut the connection, she picked up Oliver's mobile phone and erased Caroline's text message. Despicable maybe, but she wasn't going to make it easy for Caroline Prentiss to walk in and push *her* out of Oliver's life. Besides, everyone knew that phone networks weren't a hundred per cent reliable and text messages didn't always arrive. So what if Caroline was waiting for an answer? She wasn't going to get it. 'We're a family unit, and we're not splitting. For *anyone*,' she said softly.


'It's my own fault. I tripped, going down the stairs. I'll be all right when I've had a cup of tea,' Alf Varney insisted.

'You banged your head, and Betty said you were out for nearly ten minutes. That's why she called me,' Oliver said. 'And she was right. Actually, I want you to go to hospital so they can check you over properly.'

Alf folded his arms. 'I hate hospitals. At my age, once you go in, you don't come out again.'

Oliver smiled reassuringly. 'That's an exaggeration, Alf. It's not that bad.'

Alf remained stubborn. 'You know what it's like in there. Germs everywhere. There's that one that nothing can kill, that MMR.'

'MRSA,' Oliver said, trying to suppress a grin at the malapropism: the measles, mumps and rubella vaccine was a mile away from the so-called hospital 'superbug', methicillin-resistant *Staphylococcus aureus*. 'It's very rare that it actually kills someone.'

'All right. There's that one that eats people. Necri… necri…' The old man searched for the right word.

'Necrotising fasciitis,' Oliver supplied.

Alf nodded. 'That's the one.'

'It's even rarer. Alf, you need to go in for a check-up. Apart from the fact that you blacked out—'

'You've already shone a torch in my eyes and said I was fine,' Alf cut in. 'That's what they do on telly. I'm all right.'

'I'd still rather you had a proper check-up, because you were unconscious. And you've been having chest pains.'

'Have not.'

Oliver spread his hands. 'Betty told me.'

Alf scowled. 'It's none of her business.'

'She's your wife, and she's worried about you,' Oliver said gently.

Alf shrugged, still in denial. 'They don't bother me that much.'

'If they're causing you to fall down the stairs then, yes, they do.' Oliver sighed. 'The thing is, Alf, if you let them go untreated, they'll get worse. You'll feel worse. And you might end up having a full-blown heart attack—these chest pains are usually advance warning. If you have a heart attack, you'll have to stay in hospital for a while. Whereas if you go in now, let them check you over and do some tests which I can't do in the surgery, they can confirm that you have angina. Then I can give you a prescription for some drugs to stop the pain and prevent you having a heart attack.'

'What sort of tests?' Alf asked suspiciously.

'They'll hook you up to a monitor so they can see how your heart's beating—something called a twelve-lead ECG or electrocardiogram, and all that means is that there are twelve wires taped to your body which give a reading to a machine. They might ask you to walk on a treadmill for a little while so they can see what your heart does when you're exercising. They'll do some blood tests to look at your cholesterol and other blood fat, and check your blood pressure.'

'You can do that, can't you?'

'No. I don't have the right machinery to monitor what your heart's doing,' Oliver explained patiently. 'You need to go to hospital, Alf.'

'So if it *is* what you say it is…will they keep me in?'

'They'll send you home,' Oliver said. 'They'll give you some medication you can spray under your tongue when you have chest pain, and some medications you have to take every day.' Oliver decided not to tell Alf that one of the drugs was aspirin—the last thing he wanted was for the old man to self-medicate and get it wrong. 'You'll get a yearly check-up at the hospital, and you can come straight home again afterwards.'

'I hate hospitals,' Alf said again.

Back to square one. Oliver took a deep breath. He didn't want to scare Alf into going to hospital, but what other choice did he have? Unless he took the old man himself… 'How about if I go with you?' Oliver asked.

The old man brightened visibly. 'Would you?'

It could take hours, depending on how busy the emergency department was. It could well eat up the rest of Sunday. Oliver thought of Rachel. She wouldn't be pleased. But she was a doctor, too—she'd understand that sometimes you had to put your patient before yourself. 'Yes. I'll just ring Rachel and let her know what I'm doing.' He felt in his pocket for his mobile phone. It wasn't there. 'I must have left my mobile at home,' he muttered.

'You can use our phone, Dr Bedingfield,' Alf said.

'Thank you.' Oliver quickly rang home. 'Rach, it's me. I'm talking Alf Varney into hospital.'

There was a short silence, then Rachel said, 'Why you, not an ambulance?'

'I'll tell you more later.'

'Right. Any idea how long you'll be?'

'No. Don't hold up dinner for me.'

'I'll feed the kids,' Rachel said.

There was something odd in her voice. Reproach? Maybe. But what else could he do? He was the village doctor. He couldn't abandon his patients. Maybe he'd bring her some flowers home from the hospital. It wouldn't make everything right, but at least she'd know he cared…wouldn't she? 'I'll ring you before I leave the hospital.'

The wait in the emergency department seemed to take for ever, but at last Alf was checked over and everything was fine. Then, after a little intervention from Oliver, he was sent up to the cardiology department for an electrocardiogram and blood tests. Once Oliver's diagnosis was confirmed, Alf was released into Oliver's care. Oliver sorted out prescriptions for aspirin, beta-blockers and a GTN spray, got them filled at the hospital pharmacy, explained what the drugs did and the side-effects to look out for, and persuaded Betty to make sure that Alf took his medication.

So much for Sunday, he thought as he drove home. He really had intended to spend the day with Rachel. Talk to her, as Caroline had suggested last night when he'd given her a lift home and ended up staying for coffee and spilling his woes to her. She'd understood, given him the physical comfort he'd needed so badly. She'd held his hand, given him a hug, made him feel accepted.

Then he'd realised, on his way home, that he'd smelt of Caroline's perfume. And he'd been late. Very late. Rachel had been bound to leap to the wrong conclusion, he'd thought, so he'd lied and said he reeked of smoke. He hated lying to her, but what had the alternative been? She'd be so upset if she thought he'd talked about her to another woman, sharing their private concerns with someone else—and he couldn't blame her. He knew he should be talking to his wife about their problems, not Caroline, but what else could he do? Rachel was so touchy nowadays. And he went way

back with Caroline—she was the only one he could trust
with something like this.

'I thought you were going to phone from the hospital?'
Rachel asked.

'I meant to. I just…' He sighed, and handed her the flowers. 'Sorry. I got it wrong.' Just like he got *everything* wrong
these days. Rachel didn't seem that pleased with the flowers.
What would it take to make her happy? 'Alf had chest pains,
fell downstairs and blacked out. I thought it was probably
angina, but I didn't want to risk him having a full-blown
MI—' a myocardial infarction, or heart attack '—and if it
was unstable angina, he'd be in trouble. It took me a hell
of a long time to persuade him even to go to hospital—the
only way I could do it was to drive him in myself.'

'His brother died in hospital last year,' Rachel reminded
him.

'I'd forgotten about that. No wonder he's leery of the
place.' Oliver sighed. 'This isn't how I meant Sunday to
be.' His 'day off'. Except he was on call. Maybe Rachel
was right and they should put weekend and evening calls
out to a locum service. But that wasn't how the Bedingfield
Surgery worked. They'd always done the calls themselves.
A village doctor giving a proper village service. Personal.
Changing all that would be—well, like throwing it all back
in his father's face, scorning everything that his father had
worked for. He couldn't do it.

'I've given the kids their tea. I'll cook the chicken tomorrow—pasta all right with you for tonight?'

'I'm not really that hungry,' Oliver said, and immediately
wished he hadn't when that edgy look appeared in Rachel's
eyes. He backtracked fast. 'Want me to make it?'

'No. You've been out all afternoon. I'll do it.'

Oliver was too tired to argue. 'OK.'

*Just tell her*, Caroline had said. He wanted to. How he
wanted to. But now wasn't the right time.

'Mum rang,' Rachel added. 'She's coming down for a few days to help me look after Sophie. I'm picking her up from Maidstone station tomorrow afternoon—can you pick Rob up from school?'

'Uh, yes. Sure.' Actually, it wasn't convenient, but he'd call in some favours.

'That means I'll be able to do a couple of my shifts this week—you won't need your locum all the time.'

Where was this leading? Rachel definitely had a funny look on her face, but he couldn't read it. 'Rach, it's all set up now. Leave it. You might as well enjoy the break and spend some time with your mum. You don't get to see her that much.'

'Maybe I'll pop in to the surgery and have a chat with— Caroline, isn't it? About some of my patients.'

Oliver panicked. Oh, hell. The last thing he wanted right now was Caroline meeting Rachel. Because Caroline and Rachel would get on extremely well. A cup of coffee later and they'd be swapping secrets—and the last thing he wanted was for Rachel to know that he'd been talking to Caroline about their marriage problems. She'd be so hurt that he'd discussed it with someone else instead of her, even though the point was that he *couldn't* talk to her at the moment. 'Don't do that!' he said.

Rachel's eyes narrowed. 'Is there something I should know about?'

'What are you talking about?'

'What are *you* talking about?' she countered.

He didn't know. All he felt was the roaring tide of panic through his veins. He needed to keep Caroline and Rachel apart, at least for a little while. 'I've organised a locum for you this week. If you go in and start asking questions, she'll feel that you don't trust her. If she walks out, we're stuck.'

'No, we're not. I can work while Mum keeps an eye on Soph.'

Oliver raked a hand through his hair. 'Isn't the point of Ann coming here to give you a break? If you're working, you're not getting any rest. Anyway, I'm sure your mother would like to spend some time with you and the kids, not just be an unpaid babysitter.'

Rachel lifted her chin. 'She offered. I didn't ask.'

'I didn't say you did.' Why, why, *why* was this turning into a row?

*Tell her*, Caroline had said, the night of the party. If he did…he had the feeling that right now Rachel wouldn't take it well.

'Rach—'

'Forget it. I need to put these in water.' Rachel stomped into the kitchen, carrying the flowers he'd bought her as if they were poison.

Why was it all going so wrong? And were they ever going to be able to fix it?

# CHAPTER SIX

'YOU didn't answer my text,' Caroline said.

'What text?' Oliver asked.

She folded her arms. 'The one asking you if you'd told her yet.'

Oliver shook his head. 'I didn't see it. Maybe it got lost on the way to my phone—you know texts aren't a hundred per cent reliable.'

'Maybe.' Caroline didn't look convinced. 'How did it go?'

Oliver winced. 'Don't ask.'

She sighed. 'You didn't talk to her, did you?'

'I was going to, but...'

'But you wimped out.'

'I got called out.' Which wasn't the same thing—was it? He shrugged. 'Look, she's a GP. She knows how the job works. She should understand the situation, surely?'

'If she was expecting you to spend time with her at the weekend then, no, she won't understand. I wouldn't, in her shoes. Why on earth don't you use a weekend and night call-out service?' she asked.

Oliver rolled his eyes. 'Don't you start. That's what Rachel says. But this is a family practice. We've always done things this way, *always*. I can't just dump my patients on a doctor who doesn't know them.'

'It depends,' she said, 'on whether you want to stay married or not.'

'I thought you were on my side, Cally?'

'I'm not on anyone's side.' She spread her hands. 'And

I've already told you what I think. You need to get your priorities sorted out.'

'Yeah.' He took a swig of his coffee. 'I hate Monday mornings. Everyone's saved up their weekend ailments. And because it was sunny yesterday, I've got a rash of bad backs because everyone did tons of gardening without bothering to stretch or warm up their muscles properly first. I've got a huge list of test results to chase—*and* I promised Rach I'd pick Robin up, because she's meeting her mother at the train station.'

'I could pick him up for you,' Caroline offered.

Right. And by the time he got home, she and Rachel would have talked. A lot. And Rachel would be even angrier with him than she was now. Oliver couldn't face a full-blown row. The coolness between them was bad enough—he didn't want to risk making things even worse. 'No, it's OK.' Then he realised that he had the best excuse ever. 'He doesn't know who you are and we've taught him not to talk to strangers.'

'Fair enough.'

'I'll just have to shuffle my appointments about. Unless...' He gave Caroline his most charming smile. 'I don't suppose there's any chance you could cover for me this afternoon, is there?'

'Sure.' Caroline grinned. 'You big chicken. I know why you're keeping me well away from your wife, you know. And you're being very silly.'

Oliver felt his face grow hot. 'I don't know what you mean.'

But whatever Caroline was going to say, she stopped when the door opened and Prunella came in. 'Dr Bedingfield, the lab's just phoned through with the results you wanted for Megan Garner.'

'Thanks, Prunella. I'll come and get them.' Oliver smiled at the secretary. 'See you later, Cally.'

\* \* \*

Oliver was playing football with Robin in the back garden when Rachel and her mother got home.

'Daddy, Daddy! Nanny's here!'

Sophie launched herself at him, and he caught her up and swung her round. 'Hello, Princess Spotty.'

'I'm not a princess, I'm a mermaid,' Sophie informed him seriously.

'Right. Mermaid Spotty, then.'

'Mermaids don't have spots.'

'You do,' he said, kissing the tip of her nose. 'Robin, come and give Nanny Ann a big hug hello.'

Rachel's mother greeted Robin with a hug and kiss. 'You'll be as tall as your mum soon, if you keep growing at this rate!' she teased. 'Hello, Oliver.'

'Lovely to see you, Ann. Thanks for coming down and helping.'

'My pleasure.'

He got a hug and a kiss from his mother-in-law, too—so maybe Rachel hadn't told her mother that things weren't good between them. That was a relief. Having Ann in the house might reduce the strain between them, then, rather than make things worse. Or maybe Rachel *had* told her mother, and Ann had pointed out that Oliver wasn't perfect—he was doing his best but he was only human, and any marriage needed a bit of compromising here and there.

But the hugs and kisses stopped there. Rachel had already gone to put the kettle on. He sighed inwardly. If she'd just kissed him hello, he'd have felt better about things. Was it so much to ask? 'I'll take your things up, Ann.'

'Am I in my usual room?' she asked.

'Yes.' The spare room. The room that Rachel had spent yesterday evening tidying up—and when he'd asked if he could help, she'd simply snapped that perhaps he could give the children a bath for once. Oliver thought the children

were old enough to bath themselves without needing super-
vision, but had decided not to argue.

Rachel seemed less touchy over dinner. Ann was the perfect buffer, Oliver thought. He'd always liked Rachel's
mother: Ann was warm and open and had accepted him
right from the start. Unlike his own mother's attitude towards Rachel. Even the children hadn't completely mended
the fences between them.

He needed to mend a few fences himself. Only he wished
that Rachel would meet him halfway instead of expecting
him to make all the effort. 'Rach, I meant to tell you earlier—I had those test results back today. Megan's immune
to chickenpox, so there's no need to worry. I saw her in the
playground this afternoon, and told her the good news.'

'Thanks.'

Was it his imagination, or were her eyes warm again?
Please, let her be warm again. Please, he prayed.

To his pleasure, she didn't turn her back on him in bed
that night. She actually cuddled into him. Hallelujah, he
thought. Everything's going to be all right again.

And then she began stroking his thigh. He froze. They
couldn't make love, not with her mother next door! He
placed his hand on her wrist. 'Rach. We can't.'

'Why?'

'Because your mother's sleeping in the next room,' he
hissed.

She sighed. 'Oliver, it's not as if we're teenagers, needing
to creep around and pretend we're not doing anything we
shouldn't be doing. We're *married*. It's perfectly normal for
married couples to make love.'

'Even so, it doesn't feel right.'

Almost as if she guessed at the source of his embarrass-
ment, she said softly, 'We can be quiet.'

He shook his head. 'I'm sorry. It just doesn't feel right.'

She extracted her hand from his grip. 'Whatever.' She

sighed. 'Oliver, I can't remember the last time we made love.'

The accusation in her voice annoyed him. 'And that's my fault, is it? When you always go to bed early?'

She scowled. 'Says the man who spends most of his time in his study.'

'I'm the senior partner. You know I have to put the hours in to do the admin.'

'Maybe you should consider reorganising,' she said in a cross whisper.

Oh, no. Not this again. 'Dad's always run the surgery that way.'

'But you aren't your father. And, as you just said, you're the senior partner now. So surely it's up to you?'

'No, it's not. I can't just throw everything away that he's worked for.'

'I'm not asking you to throw it away! I'm just asking you to spend more time with us. The way you're carrying on, you're missing Rob and Sophie's whole childhood—and you won't get that time back.'

'You're being unfair.'

'Am I?' She shook her head. 'The other day, you said I needed evening primrose oil. Maybe *you* need Viagra.'

And with that she turned her back, making it clear that the conversation was over.

Oliver lay there, fuming. How *could* she say something like that? He wasn't impotent! He was just tired—tired from working too bloody hard to give his wife and kids a nice life, keep his parents happy and keep the whole village well. It wasn't as if he was one of those men who came home from work, sat in front of the telly and didn't move for the rest of the evening, or the sort who spent every night out at the gym and the pub with his blokey mates—he was *working*. And he wasn't to blame for their non-existent sex life.

He'd made enough overtures. Every time Rachel had re-fused them, saying she was too tired. It *wasn't* his fault.

Resentfully, he turned his back. But sleep was a long, long time coming.

'Toast?' Rachel asked as Oliver came downstairs.

'Sorry, no time for breakfast this morning.' He grabbed a banana from the fruit bowl.

She frowned. 'What's the rush? I thought surgery didn't start until half past eight.'

'It doesn't. I've got a meeting with a drug rep.'

'Right.'

'Don't bother waiting dinner for me tonight. I'll go straight from the surgery to my course. I'll get myself a pizza or something on the way home.'

'As you wish.'

Hell and double hell. She'd gone frosty on him again. But what was he supposed to do—give up his course? Make someone else see the drug reps? Oliver kissed the children goodbye and left the kitchen before he said something to Rachel he'd regret.

'Why's Daddy angry?' Robin asked.

'He's not angry,' Rachel said. Though she was. She was absolutely furious with Oliver. Her mother had come to help and he'd taken full advantage, meaning that he was spending even *more* time at work, instead of grabbing the chance to spend time with her. She forced herself to smile at her son. 'Eat your breakfast. Nanny Ann's going to take you to school today, Rob.' She busied herself making Robin's packed lunch and checking he had everything in his school-bag.

When Ann returned from taking Robin to school, she distracted Sophie with some play-dough and sat Rachel down. 'Will it help to talk about it, love?'

Rachel froze. Surely Fi hadn't told their mother about Oliver's affair? 'What did Fi say?' she asked carefully.

'Just that you were going through a bad patch. Which I can see for myself,' Ann said gently. 'You're both tired, both working too hard.'

Rachel shrugged. 'Don't tell me, tell Oliver. He doesn't think it's a problem.'

'Maybe you need some time to talk. Why don't you go out to dinner tonight? I'll look after the children. They'll be perfectly fine with me.'

'Thanks, Mum, but I can't. It's Oliver's course tonight.'

'Tomorrow, then.'

Rachel sighed. 'He'll be late home. Surgery always over-runs.'

'Then just go out later,' Ann said. 'Talk to each other. You're both tired, you're probably both snapping at each other, and resenting each other, too. Take some time out. Try and remember what you love about each other.'

'Yeah.' She loved Oliver. She just wasn't sure that he still loved her. Especially now Caroline was back. His lost love. The woman he'd never, ever told Rachel about. The secret in his past that he'd never, ever discussed with her.

When she went to pick Robin from school that afternoon, her worries increased.

'Caroline Prentiss? Really?'

Rachel knew that eavesdropping was a very stupid thing to do, that she'd only learn something she really didn't want to know, but she couldn't help herself. She listened in on the conversation.

'Yes, she saw me this morning at the surgery for my blood pressure. She looked amazing. Not a line on her face, not even the hint of a wobble under the chin. You'd never believe she was getting on for forty. She doesn't look a day over twenty-five.'

Oh, great. So Caroline Prentiss was a glamour puss. Well,

she already knew that from Ginny. It had been too much to hope for that the years had changed Caroline into someone ordinary instead of someone stylish.

'She's working at *our* surgery? I didn't think she'd come back after…well, you know,' the woman added in a whisper.

What? After Caroline had walked out on Oliver? Or after Oliver had broken her heart? I need to know, Rachel thought. I need to *know*.

She was almost at the point of turning round and talking to the mums behind her, asking them about Caroline. But then the classroom doors started opening and each child was let out as soon as the teacher saw someone was waiting for them, and the playground became the usual hubbub of shouts and laughs and screams of delight and feet thudding on tarmac, and the women behind her stopped talking about Caroline.

'Mummy!' Robin ran straight to her.

'Hello, darling.' Rachel hugged her little boy. 'Had a nice day?'

'Brilliant. We did art, and I made a puppet theatre, and…'

Rachel made all the right noises, but she wasn't really listening. All she could hear was that snatch of conversation. *She looked amazing. Not a line on her face… She doesn't look a day over twenty-five.* Rachel definitely had lines—in common with just about any woman who had small children. Lack of sleep played havoc with the blood supply to the skin below your eyes. Result—dark shadows, and lines which etched deeper with every broken night.

Whereas Caroline looked 'amazing'. Designer clothes, Rachel guessed, and time to spend on herself so she looked good. Regular workouts at the gym, facials, time for a proper haircut, time to shop so that her clothes actually matched—all the things Rachel never did. Caroline Prentiss definitely wouldn't wear her hair pulled back in a scrunchie.

And hadn't Ginny said that Caroline was the type who could look fabulous in a dustbin bag?

How on earth could Rachel compete with that? She was just…ordinary. Just like all the rest of the mums in the playground—a little tired, a little harassed, never having enough time. Being glamorous was, well, a luxury. Something reserved for birthdays and anniversaries, and even then only if she could get someone to babysit the kids to give her an extra ten minutes with her make-up.

Feeling frumpy, defeated and generally out of sorts, Rachel stomped home next to her son, still making 'mmm' and 'lovely' noises in the right places.

Oliver was late home from his course that night. Had he stopped off to see Caroline on the way home? Rachel wondered.

No. Of course not. If she started thinking like that, she'd go mad. She didn't want to become a paranoid, jealous, nagging shrew. 'Coffee?' she asked, forcing herself to smile at him.

'Thanks.'

'Soph's not asleep yet. Mum's reading her a story.'

'That's nice.'

So Oliver was treading just as carefully as she was. Rachel suppressed a sigh. How had it come to this? 'Do you want me to cook you an omelette?'

'No, I had a pizza with some of the others afterwards.'

Right. So that was why he was late.

'I did say.'

Great. And now her thoughts showed on her face. She sighed. 'I'm sorry.'

'Me, too.'

But he didn't kiss her, or even hold her. And she couldn't bring herself to make the first move. Not when he'd rejected her last night. 'Um, Mum said she'd babysit tomorrow night. Maybe we could go out to dinner.'

'I'm—' He bit back whatever he'd been going to say. 'If you like.'

'Maybe we could go to that new Italian place.'

'Sure.'

He didn't sound that thrilled by the idea. Or had he already been there with Caroline?

She pushed the thought away. 'Great. I'll tell Mum.'

'Thanks for the coffee.' And, as always, he disappeared into his office. She knew he wanted to write up his notes from his course, and she tried not to mind, but a little part of her resented it. A little part that was growing bigger and bigger each day.

# CHAPTER SEVEN

WHEN Oliver checked the lists next morning, he switched a couple of patients from Caroline's list to his own. Paula Russell, he knew, was one of Rachel's favourites, and this was a case she'd definitely want to know about this evening.

'How are you, Paula?' he asked when the thirteen-year-old walked in with her mother.

'All right, thank you, Dr Bedingfield,' she said politely.

'How's the pain?' he asked gently.

'It's bearable,' Paula said.

'Darling, I know you're being brave, but tell the doctor the truth,' Mrs Russell prompted. 'She's been pretty rough, Dr Bedingfield.'

'We've had the results of your tests back.'

'So you know what's wrong?'

Oliver nodded. 'And it's treatable.'

'Thank God,' Mrs Russell said. 'So it's not…' She closed her eyes and her voice trailed off.

'It's not leukaemia, no,' Oliver said. It was one of the conditions Rachel had managed to exclude through testing. She'd also established that the swelling around Paula's joints hadn't been reactive arthritis, swelling caused as a reaction after a virus or an infection such as Lyme disease or *Streptococcus*. Paula had come in four months ago with a limp and swollen knuckles, and when the inflammation hadn't gone down within six weeks Rachel had organised a variety of tests, including blood tests, to look at the numbers of Paula's white blood cells, red blood cells and platelets, a blood culture to check for bacteria, ESR or erythrocyte sedimentation rate to test for inflammation, and finally a test for rheumatoid factors, an antibody found in adults with rheumatoid arthritis. That test had been positive.

He smiled at them. 'It's something called JIA or juvenile idiopathic arthritis—it's called "juvenile" because it started before you were sixteen, "idiopathic" because we don't really know what causes it, and "arthritis" because your joints are inflamed.'

'I don't understand. Why don't you know what causes it?' Paula asked.

'Some doctors think it's an autoimmune disease,' Oliver said. 'Your immune system normally protects you against invaders, such as bacteria and viruses. With an autoimmune disease, your white blood cells can't tell the difference between harmful invaders and the body's healthy cells, so your immune system releases chemicals that damage your healthy tissue and makes it painful and inflamed.'

Paula's form of JIA was polyarticular, meaning that more than four joints were affected. JIA usually affected the small joints of the hands, plus weight-bearing joints such as the knees, hips, ankles, feet and neck.

'So what does it mean for Paula?' Mrs Russell asked.

'Her joints might feel warm, swollen and stiff in the morning or after she's been resting for a while, and she'll need to take very good care of her teeth. You might find that you get flare-ups sometimes, Paula—often just after you've had a virus or if you're very stressed. Flare-ups can make you feel tired and you might lose your appetite,' Oliver explained. 'You'll also need to see an eye specialist every few months to check out your eyes for something called uveitis—that's when your eye gets inflamed. Sometimes uveitis makes your eyes hurt and go red, but not always—that's why you need to go for check-ups.'

'Arthritis. It—well, it makes me sound like an old lady,' Paula said.

'Well, you're not. And there are more people than you

think with your condition,' Oliver said. 'The good news is that we can give you treatment to keep your symptoms under control and help you lead a normal, active life.'

Paula frowned. 'Does it mean I'm going to need my hips or knees replaced—like my gran?'

'Possibly, when you're a lot older,' Oliver admitted. 'But many teenagers with JIA grow out of it—the chances are two in three that you won't have any problems when you're an adult, and you're likely to be independent.'

'So what do we do in the meantime?' Mrs Russell asked. 'Do I still keep giving her the painkillers?'

'There are two strands of therapy,' Oliver said. 'The first is physical therapy. I'm going to refer you to a physiotherapist, Paula. The physiotherapist can teach you some exercises that will make you feel a lot less stiff. Some days you won't feel like doing anything other than sitting still, but your muscles have to be kept healthy so they can help support and protect your joints. The exercises will help you build up your strength, and you'll need to make sure you warm up your muscles properly before you do any exercise.' He smiled at her. 'Do you like swimming?'

'Yes.'

'Good—that's a great exercise. Walking's good, too. So's riding an exercise bike.'

Paula smiled back. 'We've got an exercise bike. It's Mum's—and it's covered in dust!'

Oliver chuckled. 'If I had one, mine probably would be, too.'

'You said there were two things,' Paula said. 'What's the other one, Dr Bedingfield?'

'Medication,' Oliver said. 'The anti-inflammatories Rachel prescribed for you obviously haven't been quite enough to control the pain, so what I'm going to prescribe for you is called a DMARD—that stands for disease-modifying anti-rheumatic drug. The one the rheumatologist suggests using is called methotrexate, and we'll try it by tablet first. You just need to take one once a week. Though there are some side-effects you need to know about. You might find you don't grow as quickly as the other girls in your class—though you *will* catch up with them—and your periods might become a bit irregular.'

Paula flushed. 'Oh.'

Oliver smiled. 'Sorry, but I'm afraid I need to embarrass you a bit more now. If you've been taking the odd sip of your mum's wine, you'll need to stop—if you drink alcohol when you're on methotrexate, you can feel quite rough and you might damage your liver. You'll also need to be a lot more careful than the average teenager when you're old enough to have sex—if you get pregnant while you're taking methotrexate, it can affect the baby.'

'I'm not having sex with anyone. I'm only thirteen,' Paula muttered.

'I know,' Oliver said kindly. Damn, he'd handled this clumsily. Rachel would have done a much better job. 'But I also know how teenage boys can put the pressure on. You've got a great excuse to say no.'

'What happens if she doesn't take them properly?' Mrs Russell asked.

'You'll get a flare-up,' Oliver said. 'So you need to take your medication regularly, Paula. And make sure you eat properly and get enough sleep, too—the healthier you are, the less your arthritis is going to affect you.'

'Right.' Paula sighed. 'Mum's always going on about what I eat.'

'Everything in moderation,' Oliver said. 'If you fancy the odd choc bar or ice cream, that's fine. Just don't stuff your face with junk food all the time—and, just as importantly, don't go on any extreme diets.'

Paula looked worried. 'Will I put on weight?'

'You shouldn't do, no,' Oliver said reassuringly. 'Oh, and

one more thing—chickenpox is doing the rounds. Have you had it?'

Paula nodded. 'When I was eight.'

It was rare to get chickenpox more than once. 'That's good.'

'Why?'

'On methotrexate, if you get chickenpox you might get it a bit more severely than normal. The medication affects certain viruses, so I can't give you a TB or polio vaccination, but you're fine to have the meningitis vaccination.'

'Does this methotrexate work?' Mrs Russell asked.

'Tests show it's safe for teenagers to use and it's effective, though it doesn't work for everyone.'

'What if it doesn't work for me?' Paula asked.

'Sometimes the tablet form doesn't work and you need to take it by injecting it under the skin instead. We'll keep a close eye on you to see how you're doing. If you need to change from tablets to injections, I can teach you how to do the injections yourself—a bit like if you were a diabetic,' Oliver said.

Paula pulled a face. 'I don't like needles very much. Is there anything else I can have instead?'

'There are other drugs, yes—but they're still being trialled at the moment. There's something called etanercept, a TNF-alpha receptor fusion protein, which looks pretty promising.' He smiled. 'And now I'm talking jargon at you. We might also need to give you something called corticosteroids—these aren't the same as bodybuilders take, so don't worry about that. What they do is reduce the inflammation and help you control the pain. Though they can have other side-effects. You might bruise more easily and your bones can become brittle, so if we give you corticosteroids you'll need to make sure you get plenty of calcium—dairy foods and sardines.'

'What about these bumps on her elbows?' Mrs Russell asked. 'Show them to Dr Bedingfield, Paula.'

Paula rolled up her sleeve to show him. 'They don't hurt or anything.'

'And they're nothing to worry about,' Oliver said when he'd examined the small nodes. 'It's part of JIA—you sometimes get small bumps and lumps on areas where there's pressure from you sitting or leaning. You might get the odd temperature every now and then, too, Paula.'

'There's an awful lot to take in,' Mrs Russell said.

Oliver nodded. 'I know, and you're bound to have a lot of questions. I've got some leaflets that might help—you can't be expected to remember everything I've said when you get home. You might find it useful to join a support group. There are a couple of national groups which have meetings locally in Maidenhead—Rachel found the local contact numbers for you.' He took the leaflets from his desk and the note Rachel had written with the telephone numbers. 'If you'd like to come and see me or Rachel in a couple of weeks, we'll see how you're getting on. You should get an appointment through the hospital to see the rheumatologist again, and also the eye specialist.' He printed the prescription, signed it and handed it to Paula. 'And if either of you are worried about anything in the meantime, or you have any questions, just give me a call.'

'Thank you, Dr Bedingfield,' Paula said. 'At least I know what's wrong with me now, so they'll shut up at school and stop saying I'm being lazy or a skiver.'

'There are some good long words in those leaflets,' Oliver said with a grin. 'Go and blind 'em with science.'

'I will,' she said, lifting her chin. 'Definitely!'

Oliver managed to get home that evening on time—purely because Caroline walked into his consulting room before he could call his next patient.

'What are you doing?' he asked in horror as she calmly logged him off the system and switched off his computer. 'I've got patients to see!'

'I'll see them. Go home,' she said.

'But—'

'But, nothing. You're supposed to be going out to dinner with your wife. So you are *not* going to work late tonight, Oliver Bedingfield. And before you fuss about who's going to lock up the surgery, *I* will. I'll drop the surgery keys off at your place on my way home.'

It was one of the most transparent excuses he'd ever heard. And he had a good answer for it, to make quite sure she didn't get to see Rachel. 'I'll lend you my spare set for tonight.'

She gave him a knowing look. 'Right. Have a nice time.'

'Yeah.'

Her voice softened. 'Oliver. Just tell her what we talked about.'

'I…' How could he? Rachel would be furious that he'd discussed her with another woman, that he'd laid bare all the private things between them. Including the fact that their sex life was less lively than a damp squib.

'Just talk to her. It'll all be fine.'

He wasn't quite so sure.

'Go.' She took his hand, pulled him out of his chair and virtually pushed him out of the room. Oliver, deciding it would be pointless to protest—particularly as he knew she was right—simply did what she suggested and went home.

Rachel was getting ready when he arrived.

'You're home early!'

Why did she look so shocked? He wasn't always late…was he? 'Cally pushed me out of the door.'

'Oh.'

His wife's face clouded. Oliver frowned. What was the matter? Surely Caroline had just done her a favour? Or was she worried that he'd been listening to his mother's usual rant about how a mother's place was in the home, not at work, and was planning to use Sophie's illness as an excuse to replace Rachel in the surgery and make her stay at home? 'Rachel, she's your locum. She's only staying as long as we need her there.'

'Right.' But Rachel didn't look any happier. Sometimes, Oliver thought, he really didn't understand his wife.

'You, um, look lovely tonight,' he said. Not that she needed make-up. He'd always thought her beautiful enough without it. Always would.

She didn't seem flattered by his comment. Suspicious, if anything. He gave up. 'I'll have a shower and see you downstairs in about fifteen minutes, OK?'

When was the last time they'd been out together without the children? Rachel wondered as they drove to the restaurant. They usually went out as a family. On the few weekends when Oliver hadn't been working—which meant any Sunday before he got called out—they'd gone to the beach or a castle somewhere, then eaten at a family restaurant. They always celebrated birthdays as a family, rather than as a couple.

Maybe they should make more of an effort. But when would they get the time? Between work, the children, Oliver's course and her PTA commitments, there wasn't much left. And she didn't like to keep asking Ginny to babysit all the time, even though she kept an eye on Ginny's son Jack sometimes in return.

It would be different if they lived in Newcastle—her mother or sister would suggest it before she could even ask them. But Oliver's family wasn't like that. Rachel had the strong impression that Isabel didn't like children very much. She tolerated the children's visits, but only just. Rob usually had his nose in a book so he was too quiet to irritate his grandmother, but Sophie was loud and would get an A+ for being demanding, attention-wise. Which was why Rachel didn't ask Isabel to babysit.

'Sophie's definitely on the mend,' Oliver said when they'd sat down and given their order to the waiter.

'She'll be back at nursery on Monday. Mum's going home on Friday afternoon,' Rachel told him.

'Right.'

For the first time she could remember, she actually felt awkward with Oliver. As if he were a stranger. Weird. They'd always been able to talk.

Until Caroline Prentiss had come back on the scene.

'I saw one of your patients today.'

She frowned. 'I thought my locum was seeing my patients?'

'She is. But I noticed that Paula Russell was on the list, and I thought you'd want to know how things were going, so I switched her over to me.' He raised an eyebrow. 'I'm not sure if she was more relieved to get a diagnosis at last or shocked to realise it's JIA. I think I embarrassed the poor kid, though—telling her about the drawbacks of methotrexate, especially when it comes to alcohol and sex.' He smiled ruefully. 'I think you'd have handled it better.'

'So I'll be the one doing the birds-and-bees talk with Rob, then?' she asked, smiling back.

'I think so. Anyway, I've told her to ring us at any time if she has questions, and I gave her the number of the local support group you found for her.'

'Thanks.' Rachel wished Oliver would show the same care to his family as he did to his patients. She thought about telling him—but something stopped her. If she told him how she felt, it might push him too hard. Worse, it might push him to Caroline. Or 'Cally', as he called her. The kind of pet name people gave to the people they loved: it was a dead give-away.

Maybe it was time she met Caroline for herself. Not a direct confrontation: she wasn't stupid enough to give Oliver an ultimatum. But maybe if they invited Caroline to dinner, it would give the other woman a chance to see Oliver at home with his wife and children. Then maybe Caroline would realise what she was asking him to give up—and maybe she'd do the right thing and leave him alone.

'We ought to have her over for dinner, you know.'

'Who?'

'Caroline.' *Cally.* The name almost stuck in her throat.

Oliver looked uncomfortable. 'Why?'

'You said yourself that you'd known her for years and she's just come back to the area. Sometimes it's difficult to fit back in again.' Though she certainly wasn't going to fit right back into her old relationship with Oliver. Not if *she* had anything to do with it. 'If she comes to dinner, it might help her feel that she's still got friends around here. Plus, it's a way of saying thank you—for stepping in for me temporarily at short notice.'

Oliver shifted in his seat. 'Mmm.'

'So why don't we?'

She could see him trying to think up an excuse. When he clearly couldn't come up with one, he sighed. 'When?'

'Saturday night.'

'She might be busy.'

'If she's only just moved back here, she probably isn't. Ask her. Or maybe I can pop in to the surgery tomorrow and have a word with her.'

There were definite signs of alarm in his face now. Was he worried that his wife and mistress were going to meet at last? Or was she just being paranoid?

'No, it's all right. I'll ask her tomorrow,' he said hastily.

'OK.'

'You do know I love you, don't you?' he asked suddenly.

'Yes.' Though she had a nasty feeling that there was a 'but' attached. What?

I love you, *but* I should have married Caroline?

I love you, *but* our marriage isn't working out?

I love you, *but* goodbye?

'I love you, too,' she said.

'Good.' He muttered something she didn't catch, though she suspected it was something like 'so that's all right, then'. Except it wasn't, was it?

The silence between them stretched out, punctuated only by the sound of cutlery against china. Although the chicken parmigiana was perfectly cooked, and Rachel adored Italian food, she found it more and more difficult to force down each mouthful. This was crazy. They were meant to be closing the gap between them, but the distance just seemed to yawn more and more as the minutes ticked by.

'So how's your course going?' she asked eventually.

'Very well.' Oliver gave her an enthusiastic run-down of what they'd done the previous evening. 'When we've finished the course, the tutor was talking about setting up a pilot scheme, using GPs trained in trauma medicine to help support the rapid response units. We're often nearer to the patients than the hospitals are, so we can get there quicker.'

She could see by his face that he wanted to do it. She wasn't surprised. Oliver had originally planned to work in emergency medicine. When Nigel had dropped out of his course in medicine, and it had become clear that it had been permanent rather than a temporary break, Oliver had felt duty-bound to switch his specialist training to general practice, for his father's sake. Rachel had wholeheartedly supported his decision to take the GP course in trauma medicine—to do something for *himself* for once. And doing support work for the rapid response units would be the nearest he'd ever come to working in the area he'd wanted to specialise in. 'Oliver, if you want to be on the pilot, you know I'll back you.'

He blinked in astonishment. 'Really?'

'Really.' Now it was her turn for the 'but'. '*But* you already work ridiculous hours. If you want to do rapid response work, you're going to have to delegate some of your other workload to make room for it. And the obvious thing is to start using a night and weekend call-out service.'

He sighed. 'We've already been through that.'

'I know. And I understand you want to keep the high levels of service that your father set. That's only natural.' She toyed with her chicken. 'But the world's not the same place it was when your father joined the practice. Our estate didn't even exist. There were half the amount of people in Hollybridge that there are now, and there wasn't the huge amount of paperwork per patient either.'

'We're a family practice.'

'And we still *will* be. We're just moving with the times. How do you think we'd cope if we still had to use a manual system for patient notes—where would we have the space to store everything? Or if you had to drive a pony and trap to house calls, instead of taking the car?'

'That's different.'

'No, it isn't.' She reached across the table and took his hand. 'Computers and cars have made our lives as doctors easier, and helped us give a better service to our patients. You're working such crazy hours that you're wearing yourself out—and you'll get to the point where you're not going to be able to give patients what they need. What's it going to take to make you realise—missing a diagnosis? Giving someone the wrong dosage? A patient dying?'

'You're being over-dramatic, Rachel.' He shook her hand off.

How to push your husband into his mistress's arms—at

breakneck speed, Rachel thought. She backed off fast. 'I'm sorry. I don't want to fight, Oliver.'

'Me neither.'

'I just want things to be…' How they used to be. Before Caroline. Well, before that even. She didn't regret having the children, not for a moment, but she did regret the pressures that were forcing her apart from Oliver.

'Me, too. Look, everything will sort itself out.'

Maybe. She just hoped it would work out the way she wanted it to be—so they didn't become a statistic.

# CHAPTER EIGHT

'RACHEL wants you to come to dinner on Saturday night,' Oliver said.

'And you'd rather I said no?' Caroline asked.

'Well.' He rubbed a hand over his face. 'It's a bit awkward.'

Caroline put her coffee mug down, walked over to him and whispered in his ear, 'Stop panicking. I'm not going to try and get Rachel alone to—'

Oliver felt the heat zing through his face. 'Um, I didn't think you would.'

She grinned. 'Yes, you did. And I suppose it is understandable.'

'It isn't that,' Oliver muttered. 'Women talk.'

'Well, that's how people communicate. Even men talk. Rubbish, most of the time, mind, but they still talk.' Caroline ruffled his hair. 'Do you think you might be going through some kind of male menopause, Ol?'

'The andropause doesn't exist,' Oliver said stiffly.

'You would say that. You're a man.' She chuckled. 'Chill out. If you're worrying that I'll tell Rachel everything you've told me, then don't. Look, I know we lost touch for a while, but we were good friends when we were younger, right?'

'Yes.' Caroline had been his girlfriend. Or so he'd thought. Until they'd been eighteen and she'd cried all over him and confessed the secret that had been eating away at her.

'And whatever you told me in confidence when we were

90

younger—you never worried then that I'd tell anyone, did you?'

'No, of course not.' Just as he'd always kept Caroline's secret. Lied for her, even.

'Nothing's changed. Now, stop worrying.' She gave him a broad wink. 'I trust I *am* allowed to bring flowers?'

'Do what you want.'

She grinned. 'If your mother invited me to dinner, I'd take her flowers. You wouldn't think anything of that, would you?'

Oliver crossed his arms and tucked his hands into his armpits so he wouldn't shake Caroline. 'Not with my mother, no.'

'So what's different about giving flowers to your wife?' She didn't wait for an answer, but sighed. 'This was why I stayed away from Hollybridge for so long. Small-town mentality. If people know who I really am…' She sighed. 'I just don't want life made difficult for my parents.'

'Would it be that bad?'

'I don't want to take the chance.' She looked bleak. 'But secrets always come out in the end.'

'I haven't said anything to anyone.' Not even Rachel. Maybe he should have told her—but, then, the secret wasn't his to tell. And it had all been in the past when he'd met Rachel, anyway.

'That's why I trusted you all those years ago. I didn't think you'd changed, but maybe you have.'

'Maybe I just don't understand women. I can't seem to make any of the women in my life happy.' Things still weren't right between him and Rachel; he'd managed to upset Caroline just now; Sophie had had a wobbly lip because he hadn't had time to read her a story that morning; and even his mother seemed to be offhand with him. Clearly he'd said or done something to upset Isabel—that, or he hadn't said or done something she'd wanted him to do. 'Why are women so complicated?'

'Chromosomes, dear,' Caroline said, patting his hand. 'Right, I've got a surgery to do.'

'Me, too.'

Flora Carson looked extremely embarrassed when she saw Oliver. 'Um, I really wanted to see the *other* Dr Bedingfield,' she said.

'I'm afraid she's off this week,' Oliver said. 'Our little girl's got chickenpox. If you'd rather see our locum, Dr Prentiss?'

Flora bit her lip. 'It's taken me ages to get the courage to come and see you. If I have to wait…'

'Maybe I can help,' Oliver said gently. 'Tell me what's worrying you.'

'It's my periods. They seem to go on for ever. And I only seem to get a week or so between them.'

'How long have they been like this?'

'Three or four months. I'm sorry to waste your time—I know you should be seeing people who are really ill—but it's just getting me down, and I'm so tired all the time.'

'You're not wasting my time at all. You're not feeling well, and that's what I'm here for,' he reassured her. 'Are your periods lighter or heavier than usual?'

'Heavier. It's a bit embarrassing, actually.' She grimaced. 'My husband made me come and see you. He's getting fed up with the fact that I'm always on. Our, um…well, you know.'

Their sex life. Yeah, Oliver knew all about non-existent sex lives. He wished he could persuade *his* wife to see someone about their little problem.

'The tiredness could be caused by anaemia,' he said. 'If your periods are long *and* heavy, it's depleting your iron stores. I'd like to take a blood sample to check your haemoglobin levels—if you're anaemic, a course of iron tablets will sort that out.' The blood test would also enable him to check for thyroid problems, which could also cause heavy periods. 'In the meantime, I'd recommend that you eat lean red meat, plenty of dark green leafy veg and drink orange juice rather than tea with your meals to help iron absorption.'

'What's causing the heavy periods?' she asked as he took the blood sample.

'Could be a few things,' he said. 'Are your periods painful at all?'

She shook her head. 'Not really.'

'That probably rules out endometriosis, where part of the lining of your womb grows in the wrong place and causes cramps. It might be fibroids or polyps. Polyps are growths in the lining of your womb, and fibroids are benign growths or swellings in the muscle of your womb,' he explained.

'Growths?' Flora paled. 'You mean cancer?'

'That's rare,' Oliver said. 'No, I mean benign lumps. Not cancer. There's also the possibility that you're coming up to the menopause early. I know you're only thirty, but sometimes in the years before you actually reach the menopause when you stop ovulating the lining in your womb gets a lot thicker before it breaks down.' He paused. 'Would you mind if I examined you, or would you prefer to come back next week when Rachel's here?'

Flora blushed. 'It's a bit embarrassing.'

He nodded. 'Don't worry, I understand. I'll make you an appointment to see Rachel then. She'll check you over—if she sees any sign of fibroids, she might refer you to the hospital for more detailed tests.'

'Will I have to have surgery?'

'If they're causing you a problem—if they hurt, or they're causing you to bleed so heavily—then, yes, we can remove them.' He paused. 'I do need to check a couple of other things with you. Is there any possibility you're pregnant?'

She shook her head. 'I'm on the Pill. And I'm bleeding so much, I can't be pregnant.'

'The Pill isn't a hundred per cent effective—there's always a tiny chance,' Oliver said. 'Sometimes a foetus doesn't travel all the way down to the womb as it should do, and implants in one of your Fallopian tubes instead— that's called an ectopic pregnancy. Eventually it'll rupture the tube, and that's very painful.' As well as being a medical emergency. 'So can I ask you to do a urine sample for me, please, and give it to Rita before you leave so I can do a test?' He handed her a sample bottle.

'Well, all right.'

'If it's positive, I'll ring you and you'll need to go straight to the emergency department,' he warned. 'Other than that, the most likely cause is fibroids or the run-up to the menopause.'

'If it's the menopause, do I have to have HRT?'

'You don't *have* to have anything,' Oliver said. 'Hormone replacement therapy's one possible treatment to help you with symptoms, but there are other options. We can talk them through together once we've established what's causing your heavy bleeding.'

'Right. Thank you.' Flora gulped. 'Well, for being understanding.'

'Any time.' He smiled at her. 'Do the sample for me, and I'll book you an appointment with Rachel. You've put up with this for long enough—we'll try and get it sorted for you as quickly as possible.'

On Friday morning, Rachel drove her mother into Maidstone, saw her off on the train and went home to blitz the house. Knowing Sophie's capacity for turning the house into a complete tip within the space of thirty seconds, she roped her daughter in to help. 'Let's have a race—see who can

make their window the shiniest! Winner gets some chocolate buttons.'

'Me, me, me!' Sophie announced, and polished her bit of
window for ages.

Oliver didn't comment that evening about how nice the
house looked, Rachel noticed. Worse still, he spent the evening in his office. Well, tough. Tomorrow he'd *have* to
spend time with her. And she was going to make quite sure
that Oliver's mistress saw a united household. The house
would be spotless, the food would be perfect, she would
look stunning and the children would be utter cherubs—
however much it cost her in chocolate buttons, Princess
Mouse stories and a new puzzle book for Robin.

'Why can't we have tea with you?' Robin asked.

'Because it's a grown-up tea. But you can read for an
extra ten minutes tonight,' Rachel said.

'You smell nice, Mummy,' he said. 'And I like your eyes.
They're all sparkly.'

Gold eyeshadow, from the posh set Fiona had given her
at Christmas as a stocking-filler. Caroline, from all accounts,
was stunning. Rachel had no intention of looking dowdy
beside her.

'You've dressed up,' Oliver said in dismay, when she
knocked on his office door and reminded him their guest
would be there in fifteen minutes, and he needed to save his
file, turn the computer off and shower.

'Well, it's not every day we have people to dinner. Maybe
we should have invited someone to partner her.'

'No, no—no need for that,' Oliver said hastily.

Well, he would say that. Caroline didn't *have* a partner.
She just had her eyes on *her* partner. Besides, Rachel and
Oliver didn't really know any single men. Except Oliver's
elder brother—and Nigel preferred his girlfriends to be in

their early twenties, so he could pretend he wasn't really forty. 'I'll just check on dinner,' she said.

As the minutes passed, Rachel grew more and more nervous. Adrenalin pumped through her, making her fingers and the back of her neck tingle. Please, please, let this work, she prayed silently. Make Caroline see that Oliver isn't right for her. Make her see that she'll ruin three lives, not just one, if she takes him from us.

When the doorbell rang, Rachel was just testing the potatoes, and the saucepan lid slipped from her hands. 'Damn, damn, damn!' she muttered, hastily retrieving it and mopping up the water from the floor. Damn. Now Oliver would be answering the door, not her.

As soon as she opened the kitchen door, she heard a small voice ask earnestly, 'Are you a fairy?'

'Sadly, no. Though I do have a friend with a magic wand.'

Oh, no. Rachel had forgotten how much Sophie liked answering the door and pretending to be the lady of the house.

'You must be Sophie and Robin, right?'

'Right,' Robin said.

'I'm Caroline.'

'You're a very important guest,' Sophie said.

'Mummy's put candles on the table. We *never* put candles on the table,' Robin added.

Never try to hide things when children are about, Rachel thought wryly. 'Not for you, sweetheart. Unless they're birthday-cake candles. This is a grown-ups' dinner, so that's why we have candles,' she said, urging the children back from the door. 'Manners, you two. If you're going to answer the door to a guest, you're supposed to let them in! Now, scoot—go and play in the play room.'

There was a chorus of 'oh' and 'but, Mummy', but eventually the children headed for the play room. Then Rachel had her first real look at The Enemy.

*The type who'd manage to look glamorous in a bin bag.*
Ginny had been understating things just a tad, Rachel
thought. Caroline was indeed tall, slim and pretty, with long
blonde hair styled to frame her face and flatter her to per-
fection, intensely blue eyes and a charming smile. Her dress
was clearly a designer number, beautifully cut in gorgeous
fabric. No wonder Sophie had thought her a fairy. She
looked absolutely stunning.

Rachel's heart sank. She'd made an effort, really tried,
and she needn't have bothered. Next to Caroline Prentiss,
she looked positively dowdy. She might just as well have
scruffed around in tracksuit bottoms and a baggy T-shirt,
scrubbed her face shiny and kept her hair in a scrunchie.
'Do come in,' she said.

'Thank you.' Caroline's smile was full-wattage and, even
though Rachel wanted to push her off a cliff, she couldn't
help responding. 'It was so kind of you to invite me—and
I know it was you who invited me. It wouldn't have oc-
curred to Ol.'

*Ol?* Nobody shortened Oliver's name, ever!

But, then, he and Caroline went back a long, long way.
Longer than he and Rachel did.

Tough. He'd chosen Rachel. She'd make sure Caroline
realised that tonight.

'Well, it must be difficult, coming back to your old home
town. Everyone's changed. Besides, it's a sort of thank you
from me as well—for standing in for me this week.'
Hopefully Caroline would take the hint: as of next week,
*she* would be back at the practice. And she had no intention
of moving her job or her home to suit Caroline Prentiss.

'It was a pleasure. I hope I've left a decent set of notes
for you, but if I haven't and you want me to explain anything, just ring me—Ol knows my number.'

I just bet he does, Rachel thought.

'Would you like a drink?' she enquired sweetly. A cocktail, perhaps. Arsenic Surprise with a sprinkle of cyanide for good measure.

'I'd love one.'

'We've got some white wine in the fridge, or I can open a bottle of red.'

'White would be lovely, thanks.' Caroline handed her a huge bunch of peonies. 'I'll admit now, I pinched these from Dad's garden—but as he and Mum went on holiday for a fortnight this afternoon, I'm sure he'd rather someone actually appreciated them. They won't last long with me—I've got brown thumbs,' Caroline added with a grimace. 'I water the things, I even talk to them, and it doesn't make a bit of difference. Two days, and the whole garden's brown.'

'Right. Er, thank you. I'll put them in water.'

'Anything I can do to help?'

Apart from leave my husband alone? Rachel wanted to ask. 'No, it's fine.'

'Mind if I tag along?' Caroline followed Rachel into the kitchen. 'I brought this as a contribution for tonight, too.' She set a bottle on the worktop. 'Ol, of course, is completely hopeless—didn't give me a clue as to whether you wanted red or white. Men! So I played it safe.'

With an expensive bottle of New Zealand sauvignon blanc. Caroline might be a cold-hearted cow, Rachel thought, but she had good taste in wine.

'I brought the kids something, too, but I thought I'd check with you before I hand over any goodies.' She handed Rachel a carrier bag in exchange for a glass of wine.

'Do you have children of your own?' Rachel asked.

'No. I'm afraid I took a bit of a guess, based on friends' children. I've heard that all little girls under four adore anything pink, and boys like things they can build.'

The tiara and feather boa were absolutely Sophie, and Robin would adore the build-your-own-spaceship kit. Was this Caroline's way of buying her way into the children's affections? Rachel forced herself to be pleasant. 'Thank you. They'll love them.'

'Good. I can remember as a child getting presents I *hated*, and I always had to be polite and grateful when I really wanted to ask if I could have a book rather than a doll next time, please.' Caroline smiled. 'Luckily my friends usually give me a list of suggestions for Christmas and birthday presents for their littlies. I wouldn't have a clue otherwise.'

'Would you like to give them to them? I'll go and see why Oliver's taking so long upstairs.' Subtext: *my* husband. *My* bathroom. *My* bedroom.

'Men claim they don't take as long as women in the bathroom—that's only because they take *longer*,' Caroline said with a grin.

Damn. Not only was she glamorous, she was witty as well. In fact, Rachel thought as she hurried upstairs, if it wasn't for the fact that Caroline was trying to steal her husband, she'd actually *like* the woman.

'Oliver, she's here. Will you hurry up?' she muttered through the *en suite* door.

'Thirty seconds,' Oliver called back. 'Promise.'

It was more like five minutes, but at last he appeared, looking handsome, gorgeous—and Rachel definitely had the feeling he'd made the effort for Caroline's sake, not hers.

Well, she wasn't going to make a scene. She was just going to be super-nice. And hopefully Caroline would feel so guilty that she'd leave Oliver alone in future.

'Right, you two. Bedtime,' she said to the children.

'But I want to wear my crown!' Sophie protested.

'And I want to make my spaceship!' Rob said, his bottom lip mutinous.

'OK, as it's Saturday, you can stay up a bit longer—in your bedrooms. Daddy will be up later to read you a story, Soph—that's *one* story—and turn out the lights,' she warned.

'Love you, Mummy,' Sophie said, hugging her and kissing her. 'Love you, Daddy.'

Rob followed suit, then both of them stood looking at Caroline.

'Goodnight, Princess Fairy. Goodnight, Astronaut Bedingfield,' Caroline said solemnly.

They beamed, and hugged her. Rachel's heart wrenched. She hadn't wanted Caroline to be vile to the children—but she hadn't wanted the children to be a complete pushover either!

Silently, she put the first course on the table. And then suddenly it was just the three of them, and the dining room seemed far too small.

'This is very nice, Rachel. You've gone to an awful lot of trouble,' Caroline said of the home-made smoked salmon mousse.

'I like cooking,' Rachel said.

Caroline grinned. 'I detest it. After years of being forced to bake cakes and cut prissy little sandwiches for vicarage garden parties, I swore I'd never, ever cook again. I'm the Queen of Ready Meals. But don't tell any of the patients, or they'll never listen to me when I bang on about watching the amount of saturated fat they eat and reducing their salt intake.' She winked.

Good. That was one area where she'd score higher than Caroline, then: Oliver liked Rachel's cooking. She made a mental note to pull out all the stops over the next few weeks. Remind him what he'd be giving up.

The second course went down just as well. 'Don't tell me you grow your own herbs as well,' Caroline said. 'That's tarragon in the sauce with the chicken, yes?'

Rachel nodded. 'Though I'll admit I bought the fresh herbs from the supermarket.'

'Much easier. I would, if I ever cooked.' Caroline gave

a sigh of bliss. 'Minted Jersey Royals. That's when I always know it's summer.'

Why did Caroline have to be so nice? Why couldn't she have been a horrible, nasty piece of work? Not that Rachel wanted Oliver to spend the rest of his life with someone who made him miserable. She just wanted him to be happy. Preferably with her.

'So you two were friends for years, then?' Rachel asked.

'Mmm. We both went to the same school.'

Weren't vicars supposed to be poor? How come Caroline's parents had been able to afford private education?

'She's cleverer than me. Got a scholarship,' Oliver said.

Rachel flushed, hoping that her thoughts hadn't been completely readable.

'That's why she went to Oxford, not London,' he added.

'A medical degree's still a medical degree, wherever it came from. And it's how you treat your patients that counts,' Caroline corrected him.

Rachel's thoughts exactly. Hell. Why did Caroline have to be in tune with her? Why couldn't she be a prissy, cold-hearted snob? Surely that was the sort of woman Isabel Bedingfield would have wanted for her son: a woman out of the same mould as her own?

'We lost touch a year or so after I went to Oxford. I had a bit of, um, well, a breakdown, really,' Caroline explained. 'And I didn't want to come back to Hollybridge.'

Why? Because she'd split up with Oliver? And why *had* she split up with Oliver? Had it been anything to do with her 'breakdown'?

'What made you change your mind?' Was it because she wanted Oliver back? Rachel had to know.

'After I qualified, I travelled a bit,' Caroline said. 'I spent some time in the States, then went to Australia. I worked in Sydney for a few years.'

Well, that would explain why she hadn't come to the wedding.

'I half thought about settling out there for good.' She grimaced. 'But being a vicar's daughter means you get this strict sense of duty—sort of through osmosis. Dad's getting near retirement, and Mum's not been so well lately, so I thought I'd better show my face again. I applied for a locum registration, caught the plane back and here I am again.'

'And are you staying?'

'Maybe. I'm using the time while Mum and Dad are on holiday to look for a place of my own.'

Just as long as it's not this one, Rachel thought.

'You're from Newcastle, aren't you?' Caroline asked.

'Yes.'

'That's a part of the world I haven't been to. Though I've heard the scenery up there's amazing. Castles and light-houses—and Holy Island, of course.'

'There are plenty of castles in Kent,' Rachel said.

'Mmm, but it's not the same. Kent's pretty flat—and covered in motorways.'

It sounded as if Caroline didn't really want to stay around here. Oliver wouldn't go with her, Rachel knew—if nothing else, his loyalty to the practice would keep him in Hollybridge.

'I'll, um, get pudding,' Rachel said when the silence had stretched just that little bit too long.

'I'll help you bring the things out,' Caroline said.

Odd. Shouldn't she be looking for any excuse to be on her own with Oliver? And why did Oliver have that panicky look in his eyes? Maybe I've drunk too much wine, Rachel thought.

'That looks incredibly full of calories,' Caroline said as Rachel took the pudding from the fridge.

'Sorry, are you dieting?'

Caroline scoffed. 'Not on your life. I was thinking of Ol.'

'What about me?' Oliver demanded as they returned to the dining room.

'I saw your brother the other day. He's definitely spreading round the middle. You'll be next. So really, if Rachel and I eat your share of this, we'll be doing you a favour.' Caroline let Rachel help her to a large amount. 'Oh. This is to die for,' she said after the first taste.

'White chocolate mousse,' Rachel said.

'And raspberries to take the edge off the sweetness. Perfect.'

'Do you really think I'm spreading round the middle?' Oliver asked.

Caroline shrugged. 'You tell me.'

Didn't she *know*? Hadn't she been…well…close enough to Oliver's naked body to notice?

Caroline had second helpings of the pudding. And when Rachel brought in the coffee and cannoli wafers, Caroline snapped her fingers. 'Rats. I knew there was something I meant to bring.'

Rachel frowned. 'What?'

'Tim Tams. Aussie chocolate biscuits,' Caroline explained. 'You have to drink coffee through them, then eat them quickly before they collapse. Dad would have a fit, saying it's bad manners, but it's really the best way to eat them. The Aussie way.' She grinned. 'Maybe I can tempt you over to have lunch with me one day next week, and you can try them for yourself.'

'What about me?' Oliver asked.

'This is chocolate. Women's stuff,' Caroline admonished him. 'So, how about it, Rachel? Or shall I call you Rach?'

'Er—I don't really get a chance for lunch. You know, with picking Soph up from nursery and meeting Rob from school.'

'Bring Sophie with you. The house is very child-friendly; Mum's got a box of toys.'

'Well...thanks.' She'd find a polite excuse nearer the time.

By the end of the evening, Rachel thought that in other circumstances she would have liked Caroline. But then Oliver saw Caroline to the door. And he was gone for *ages*. Rachel couldn't help peeking through the kitchen door, and she regretted it instantly. Caroline and Oliver were talking very quietly—and standing so close together that you could barely have got a blade of grass between them.

Oh, Oliver. How can you possibly do this, in *our* house, with our children asleep upstairs? Rachel thought.

But she wasn't giving up on her marriage yet. Not by a long way. Caroline might be nice—but Rachel wasn't going to hand over her husband on a silver platter. Now she knew what the competition was, she could start to do something about it.

# CHAPTER NINE

ON MONDAY morning, Rachel dropped the children at school and nursery and walked into the practice. Her consulting room was exactly as she'd left it, with a framed photograph of Oliver and the children on her desk and the walls decorated with a lion made out of Sophie's handprints and a robot painted by Robin when he'd first started school.

The one thing Caroline had left—in extremely neat handwriting—was a list of the patients she'd seen. Rachel flicked through the computerised notes on the first couple and knew she wouldn't have to bother reviewing the rest. Caroline's notes were concise yet detailed enough so that Rachel would be able to follow exactly what she'd done.

If only you didn't have your sights set on my husband, Rachel thought. We could have been friends.

Surgery went quickly—the usual Monday morning aches and pains which had got worse over the weekend, a couple of infected splinters, a bad back and a sprained ankle. And then Flora Carson came in.

'Hello, Flora.' Oliver had already filled Rachel in on the situation. 'Come and sit down. How are you feeling?' Rachel asked.

Flora tried to smile, but admitted, 'Pretty grim.'

Rachel checked her file. 'Right. Oliver's managed to push through your blood tests, and your haemoglobin's lower than it should be. You're anaemic, so I'm going to prescribe some iron tablets—they'll go a long way to making you feel less tired and run down.'

'Believe me, I ate a ton of spinach over the weekend,' Flora said feelingly.

Rachel grinned. 'Rather you than me! The urine sample showed you're not pregnant, so that's one complication out of the way. Oliver thinks you might have fibroids, so would you mind if I examined you?'

'I know I should have let Dr Bedingfield do it last week. I just felt too…well, embarrassed,' Flora explained.

'It's not a problem. Periods aren't the easiest things to discuss with men. He knows the theory, but…at the end of the day, he's a man. He's never actually *had* a period.'

To her relief, Flora seemed to relax. 'Would you like to lie down on the couch for me?' She examined Flora's abdomen. 'Sometimes you can feel fibroids, if they're very big. I can't feel anything, so I need to do an internal exam. Is that all right?'

Flora nodded.

'Have you noticed if you've needed to wee more often lately?'

'If anything, it's the other way round.'

Which could mean that the fibroid—if it *was* a fibroid— had pushed the neck of the bladder upwards and elongated the urethra. 'OK. Tell me if anything feels uncomfortable or tender, and I'll stop straight away,' Rachel said. The internal exam showed exactly what she'd expected: Flora's uterus was firm and enlarged in places. There was no tenderness either. 'It feels like a fibroid to me, but I'd like to send you to hospital for a scan to confirm it and rule out any other problems.'

'A scan?' Flora looked worried.

'Fibroids are benign tumours—they're not cancerous,' Rachel reassured her. 'The scan's a bit like you'd have if you were pregnant, and it'll show how many fibroids you have and how big they are.'

'You can have more than one?'

'Yes—and they can vary from the size of a pea to the size of a melon,' Rachel explained. 'It's pretty common, actually: around one in five women over the age of thirty have fibroids.'

'How did I get it?'

Rachel shook her head. 'We don't know why fibroids develop—it's basically when the smooth muscle cells grow too much. Some people are more prone than others.'

'So what do I do now?'

'If it wasn't causing you problems, I'd say leave it—fibroids usually shrink after menopause. But in your case, you're already having problems and you've got another fifteen years or so before you should be reaching menopause. It really depends on the size of the fibroids,' Rachel said. 'If they're not too big, you might be able to take some tablets—something called tranexamic acid, which reduces the blood clots in your uterus and makes your period lighter.'

'So I won't have to have surgery?'

'As I said, it depends. If the fibroids are big, there are three surgical options,' Rachel said. 'You're still young, so you might want to have children—in that case the surgeon will suggest a myomectomy, which means they'll just remove the fibroid. If you were over forty and you'd already had a family, the surgeon might suggest a hysterectomy, or there's a new technique called uterine artery embolisation. That's where the surgeon can put a catheter—that's a very thin flexible tube—into an artery in your leg. Then he'll inject a chemical which will block some of the arteries in your uterus—that cuts off the blood supply to the fibroid and makes it shrink. But we don't know what the long-term effects will be, so you'll need to discuss it fully with the surgeon before you make any decisions.'

'Thanks, Rachel. I wish I'd come earlier. It's been really coming between Colin and me—I always seem to be on, so I'm never in the mood for making love nowadays.'

Yeah. I know someone who's like that, Rachel thought.

Except he didn't have long, heavy periods to drain his energy. Oliver didn't actually have an excuse—apart from the fact he was obviously getting his needs met elsewhere. 'At least you're doing something about it now.' Which was exactly what she needed to do—something to get her love life with Oliver back on an even keel. Something to make him realise that they still had a lot going for them, and that Caroline should stay where she'd come from. In the past.

'I'll refer you for a scan and a consultation with the specialist, and you should hear something from the hospital this week,' Rachel said. 'It's easy for me to say, but try not to worry. And if you've got any questions, just give me a call.'

When Flora left, Rachel considered nipping in to see Oliver and trying to persuade him to have lunch with her—but she knew he didn't really have the time and, besides, she needed to go and pick Sophie up from nursery. Maybe tonight they'd get a few minutes of quality time together.

Maybe.


Oliver flicked into his texts and grinned as he saw the message: *She's lovely—you're a lucky man.*

Yeah. He knew that. His smile faded. *I know. But.*

A few seconds later, the reply came zinging back. *You need to talk to her. Don't let her slip through your fingers, you idiot.*

Yeah, he knew that, too. But *how*?

*Tell her the truth. Tell her how you feel.*

He'd tried, but the words just wouldn't come out. *I'm hopeless with words. When it really matters.*

*Maybe I can help. Let me think about it,* she texted back.

Half an hour later, Oliver's phone buzzed discreetly in his pocket. As soon as his patient had gone, he checked his phone.

*I've loved you since the moment I first set eyes on you. I knew you were the one I wanted to grow old with. That hasn't changed and it never will. I love you.*

He smiled. *That's perfect*, he replied. He had the words now. All he had to do was find the right time to tell Rachel.

Rachel had just made Sophie a sandwich when the phone rang. Her sister, probably, to see how things were—ringing at a time when she knew Oliver wouldn't be there so Rachel could talk freely. 'Hi,' she said.

'Hello, Rachel.'

Rachel recognised the voice and the back of her neck started to knot up. Caroline. Not Fiona.

'I just wanted to ring and say thank you for Saturday. I enjoyed it so much.'

'Pleasure,' Rachel lied. Oh, hell. She wanted to tell Caroline to leave her husband alone and go to hell—but would a direct confrontation make things worse? With Oliver, it was always best to take a softer, more oblique approach. If she rocked the boat now, there was a very good chance that she'd fall out. She took a deep breath. Stay calm, she reminded herself. Pretend you know nothing. 'Thanks for looking after my patients so well.'

'I enjoyed it. It's a nice practice to work in.'

Yes, but you're not coming back to it, Rachel thought. You're not taking my place at work *or* at home.

'Um, I was wondering if you were free for lunch on Thursday?'

She hadn't expected that. Surely Caroline had just been socially pleasant on Saturday when she'd suggested having lunch together? The kind of thing you said to be polite but didn't really mean? 'I'm not sure,' Rachel hedged. And then she came up with the ultimate in cowardly excuses. 'And, um, I'm in the middle of doing Sophie's lunch.'

'Oh, I'm so sorry! That's the thing about not having children. You have no idea of their routines. Tell you what, I'll pencil it in. Let's say half past twelve. If it's not convenient, give me a bell and let me know when's a better time, OK?'

Like never. 'OK,' Rachel said.

'Speak to you soon, then.' And the line went dead.

The woman's unbelievable. How can she possibly try to make friends with me when she's planning to go off with my husband? Rachel thought, gritting her teeth. Now she'd have to find some kind of excuse before Thursday.


'Oliver—I know it's a bit of a cheek, but I wondered if you could do me a favour?' Tara asked, smiling shyly at him. 'That bit about cricothyroidotomy Keith covered tonight— I just didn't get it. And you always seem to, well, grasp things better than anyone else.'

'I'm sure if you ask, he won't mind going through it again.'

'I feel so *stupid*, having to ask. I mean, I'm a qualified GP. It's not as if I'm a wet-behind-the-ears house officer! I should have a better idea of things. Anyway, I was think-ing…look, if I buy you a pint, would you mind taking me through it?'

'Um, well, I'm driving, so I can't drink.'

'An orange juice, then.'

He knew that half the people on the course usually went for a drink afterwards. He didn't usually bother—simply because he felt too guilty, aware that he was already out on a Tuesday evening for the course and Rachel never had a night off from the children. It felt too selfish somehow. 'Um…' How could he say no, but do it nicely without mak-ing Tara feel he was being standoffish? And she *had* asked for his help. If he did have a drink with Tara, it wouldn't be as if he was going out with another woman. It was simply helping a colleague on the course. 'OK. But it'll have to be a quick one, I'm afraid.'

'Thank you, Oliver. It's so *kind* of you.' She beamed at

him, and slipped an arm through his. 'We normally go to the Jolly Sailors, but it's a bit noisy there. It might be better if we went somewhere quieter, where we can spread our papers out a bit and I can actually hear you.'

'Sure.' He smiled back at her. 'Let's go.'

Had something happened? He was normally back way before now, Rachel thought. Maybe there had been some sort of traffic jam and he'd been held up. Maybe an accident— and, knowing Oliver, he'd gone to help until the ambulance arrived. Maybe... She damped down the feeling of unease. No. Of course Oliver wouldn't have been in an accident.

She forced herself to concentrate on the journal she was reading. And when she heard Oliver's key in the lock, she didn't jump up and rush to him. The last thing she should do right now was be clingy. That would be the quickest way to drive him away.

'Good session tonight?' she asked.

'Yeah. Keith covered airway obstructions tonight—intubation, jaw thrust and needle cricothyroidotomy. It was interesting stuff.'

'Glad you enjoyed it.' She uncurled from the sofa and went to kiss him hello. And then her nostrils flared as she recognised the scent clinging to his skin.

*Caroline's* scent.

So that was why he'd been late.

Then a really nasty thought hit her. Had he even gone to his course? Had he gone to see Caroline instead? For all she knew, the course could have finished. Maybe he'd been lying to her all along—maybe he wasn't even doing a term's course. Advanced trauma and life support courses were often held over the course of three days. Why hadn't Oliver booked himself on one of those intensive sessions and brought in a locum to cover him? Did the course even exist?

But how could she ask him? How would she even know

that he was telling her the truth? Her marriage was disintegrating fast around her, and she had no idea how to stop it or what to do next. It felt as if her blood had frozen, right through to the marrow. She couldn't move, couldn't do anything.

'Are you all right?' Oliver asked.

'Fine. Just a bit tired,' Rachel lied. *Just that my heart's breaking and I don't know how to stop you leaving me.*

'I'll go and have a shower.'

*What, to wash the scent of your mistress from your skin? You should've thought of that before you came home,* Rachel thought bitterly. 'Fine.'

Oliver walked upstairs. Amazing. He'd been over an hour late, and Rachel hadn't even noticed. She hadn't said a thing. He could have stayed out all night, he thought bitterly, and she wouldn't have noticed. It was as if she really didn't care any more.

*I've loved you since the moment I first set eyes on you. I knew you were the one I wanted to grow old with. That hasn't changed and it never will.* But it wasn't true for her any more, was it?

He sighed. How stupid he'd been. He'd thought that if he didn't say anything, didn't rock the boat, they'd get through this bad patch. But it just seemed to go on and on and on, and every day their marriage was falling further apart.

He scrubbed himself in the shower. Maybe if they made love, everything would be all right. Maybe what they needed was to connect again—skin to skin, just the two of them, nothing to distract them from each other. Just for a little while.

As he'd half expected, Rachel was in bed when he came out of the bathroom. Reading a journal.

He slid under the covers next to her. 'How was your day?'

She kept her eyes firmly fixed on the journal. 'OK.'

She didn't sound that enthusiastic. And, he noted in dismay, she was wearing pyjamas. Well, he wasn't going to let that put him off. He wanted to lose himself in her body, let her lose herself in him. And then he'd tell her how much he loved her. Tell her how he really felt. And then maybe everything would be all right.

He snuggled up beside her. 'Rach.'

'Mmm?'

He slid his fingertips under the hem of her pyjama top. 'Your skin's so soft.'

She pushed his hand away. 'No. We can't.'

'Why not?'

'Wrong time of the month.'

'Oh.' Whoever said that disappointment was a sinking feeling hadn't said the half of it. It felt more like being sucked straight down the plughole. Still, at least it explained why she'd been a bit strained with him for the last few days. Premenstrual syndrome. Though she never used to have it that badly. What can I do to make you love me again, the way you used to? he wondered.

'Maybe…' he began cautiously.

'What?'

This time she looked at him. And her eyes were very, very cold. Oliver gave up. 'Nothing,' he said, and reached over to his bedside table for his own journal.

On Wednesday morning, Rachel was up early. She was making Robin's packed lunch for school when she noticed that Oliver's mobile phone was lying on the kitchen worktop. His phone was the same as hers. It would be all too easy for them to take the wrong phones—they'd done it before. Before she had time to think about what she was doing, she'd taken her phone from her handbag and swapped it with Oliver's.

She tried to put it out of her mind until she'd dropped the children off. Then, in the surgery car park, she checked Oliver's text messages. There was one from 'C', dated Monday morning. Knowing even as she did it that this was stupid, the worst mistake she could make, she opened it.

*I've loved you since the moment I first set eyes on you. I knew you were the one I wanted to grow old with. That hasn't changed and it never will. I love you.*

She read the message five times before its meaning sank in.

Caroline was still in love with Oliver.

And Oliver clearly felt the same way about Caroline. Why else would he have saved the message rather than deleting it?

'You lying, cheating, devious *bastard*!' Anger rolled through her, a fury she'd never known before. She had proof now. Oliver was cheating on her and he wasn't even trying to hide it. He was going to throw away everything they had, uncaring about how it affected the children or his wife. What right did he have to smash their world into little tiny pieces, throw fourteen years of her life away?

She dropped the phone, clenched her fists to stop them shaking and banged both hands on the steering-wheel, hard, taking out her anger and frustration on an anonymous lump of plastic and metal and wishing that she was slugging Oliver instead.

When the car horn blared out, she jumped in shock. Hell. She'd forgotten that the hooter was in the middle of the steering-wheel.

She flexed her hands. They hurt. Damn. She'd hit the steering-wheel so hard she could have fractured her wrists. But the pain was dull, throbbing: she could cope with it. Unlike the knifing pain inside. It felt as if someone had ripped her chest open, gripped her heart and was slowly squeezing every drop of blood from it. Squeezing every drop of love Oliver had ever given her and letting it gurgle down the drain.

What the hell was she going to do?

If she confronted him, he'd leave. She'd lose him for good.

If she didn't confront him...he might leave anyway. Or if this affair burned itself out, he'd think he could do it again and again, because Rachel was too spineless to stand up for her marriage.

And what about the kids? They loved Oliver. Even if he didn't give them as much attention as Rachel did, they adored him. Looked up to him. Hungered for his rare words of praise—you could see it in the glow of their faces when he'd told them they'd done something well. She couldn't possibly cut them off from him. But if Oliver tried to take the children from her... God, even the thought of it was unbearable. She knew she wouldn't survive the reality.

She closed her eyes, letting her head drop forward onto the steering-wheel. Somehow she had to find the strength to walk into the surgery. Walk into the consulting room next to her husband's. Pretend that her heart hadn't broken into jagged little shards. Listen to her patients, care for them, put the mess of her marriage out of her mind until after surgery.

And then, somehow, she had to decide what to do. Whether to fight for her marriage—for the man she loved—or whether she should face facts and realise it was time to let him go.

Either way, she lost.

# CHAPTER TEN

SOMEHOW, Rachel managed to pin a smile on her face and convince the world that nothing was wrong—at least, nobody asked her what the matter was. Oliver spent the evening working, and for once, she found it a relief instead of a trial. Until she worked out what to do, she didn't really want to be on her own with him. The last thing they needed was a confrontation, where they'd both say something in the heat of the moment that they'd regret later—something that might blow their whole relationship wide apart.

Crazy. In every other area of her life she knew what to do—or knew that she could cope with things going wrong and could fix things. Where her marriage was concerned, she'd somehow become this pathetic, timid little creature who was afraid to say or do the wrong thing.

Probably because Oliver mattered more to her than anything else. If you failed an exam you could resit it; if you dented the car, you could get it fixed. But if your marriage broke down, the chances were that you couldn't make it work again. She just had to take things slowly, carefully and hope they'd come out of this bad patch together rather than apart.

On Thursday morning Rachel had to tell Michael Finch some bad news. 'How are you feeling?' she asked as he sat down.

'OK.' Though Rachel could see he was having trouble breathing.

'I've had the results back for your chest X-ray and the lung function tests.'

116

'When I breathed into that machine at hospital, you mean?'

She nodded. 'And I'm sorry, it's not good news.' The results weren't good. The X-ray showed widespread shadowing and 'eggshell' calcification—thin streaks of calcium deposits—around the hilar lymph nodes. The spirometer results showed that Michael's breathing was definitely restricted.

'I've got cancer?' he asked.

She shook her head. 'It's something called silicosis—an industrial lung disease. You may have heard of "potter's rot", "grinder's rot" and "stonemason's disease".'

'Potter's rot, yes.' He frowned. 'They used to get that years ago.'

'Cases are much rarer nowadays, because working practices are a lot safer—but it still takes years for the disease to show up,' Rachel said. 'People get it when they work with silica, which is in sandstone, granite, coal and silica sand. So foundry workers, sandblasters and potters are most at risk.'

'I used to be a potter.' Michael frowned. 'I did dry-finishing. But I changed my job fifteen years ago.'

'Once you've got it, it gradually gets worse—even after you've stopped working with silica,' Rachel explained gently.

'So I've probably had it for years?'

She nodded. 'What happened is that you breathed dust into your lungs and the dust contained silica—which is about ten times worse than coal. If you've got thirty grams of coal dust in your lungs, you might get away without too many problems, but just three grams of silica can make you feel very ill. When the silica reaches the lining of your lungs, it makes them inflamed, and over time this inflammation turns into thickened, scarred tissue—it's a process called fibrosis.'

'Am I going to die from it?'

'Not in the immediate future,' Rachel reassured him.

'But there's no cure?' Michael guessed.

'No. But I can make you more comfortable. The damage to your lung tissue means your lungs can't supply your blood with oxygen as well as they should do. So that's why your chest feels tight, you're short of breath when you walk and you've had that nasty cough.'

'Even though I'm not bringing anything up?'

'Even though you're not bringing anything up,' she confirmed. 'I can give you something to reduce the inflammation which will help you breathe more easily. But you're also more likely to get chest infections, and you're vulnerable to TB. I'd recommend that you have a flu jab every year, plus a vaccination against pneumococcal infection, which is one of the most common causes of pneumonia. Do you smoke at all?'

'No. I gave up twenty years ago.'

'Good—because smoking will make your symptoms worse and will also speed up the progress of the disease.' She paused. 'The good thing is that you're not exposed to silica any more. You can claim compensation under the Industrial Injuries Act—I can get some forms sent to you, and I can help you fill them in if you like.'

'Thank you.' Michael shook his head. 'Sorry, I can't really take this in. So when I was a potter, my job ruined my lungs?'

'I'm afraid so.'

He bit his lip. 'I'm retiring this year. Peg and me, we were going to go to Australia and see her cousins.'

'You can still go.'

'But if I can't breathe properly… I thought this was just a chest infection and it'd clear up with antibiotics. Or that it was asthma or something.'

'I'm sorry, Michael.'

'How long have I got?'

'We can't tell. All we can do is keep a close check on you and give you regular X-rays.'

He stared at the floor. 'I don't know how I'm going to tell Peg.'

'She'll probably have a few questions, so if you'd like me to be there when you tell her, I can do that.'

'Thanks, Doc. It's just…I wasn't expecting this.'

'I know, and it's a horrible shock.'

'Peg and me, we'd better make the most of every moment, then.' He swallowed hard. 'I'll, um, ask Rita to make us an appointment, shall I?'

'That's fine. Try and get her to squeeze you in for tomorrow.' Rachel smiled sympathetically at him and printed out a prescription. 'This is for an inhaler—pretty much the same as you'd use if you had asthma. It'll help reduce the inflammation in your lungs and make it easier for you to breathe. I'll also send you for regular chest X-rays so we can keep an eye on what's happening.'

'Right.'

'If you find that breathing's harder than usual, I want you to come straight here and see me so I can check out if you have a chest infection and give you something to clear it up. I won't think you're being a nuisance—and if you leave it, you'll feel really rough,' she warned.

'Message received, Doc.' He gave her a rueful smile. 'I think I need to see Peg. Tell her I love her. It's things like this that make you realise what's really important in life, isn't it?'

'Yeah. You take care.' Rachel swallowed the lump in her throat as he left her consulting room.

Supposing it had been Oliver seeing his GP and discovering that he had industrial lung disease? She couldn't bear the idea of him suffering. Or, worse, losing him.

Seeing Michael had confirmed what her heart had known

all along. She loved Oliver. She didn't want to lose him. Their marriage was definitely worth fighting for, so she was going to beat Caroline at her own game and make Oliver fall back in love with her and out of love with Caroline. If Oliver wanted someone more glamorous and less mumsy, then that was exactly what he'd get. Rachel wasn't going to confront him and make demands: she was going to let him choose for himself, so he'd stick with his choice and never regret it.

And she'd make absolutely sure that *she* was his choice, not Caroline.

She picked up the phone, switched to an outside line and dialled the other woman's number. To her relief, the vicarage answering machine clicked on. 'It's Rachel,' she said. 'I'm sorry, I won't be able to make lunch today.' Lying wasn't something that Rachel approved of. But sometimes you needed to bend the rules, and now was one of those times. 'I've got a headache and I'm feeling rotten. Perhaps we can make it another day?' Not that there'd ever be another day.

Luckily Thursday was Sophie's full day at nursery and Rachel had the afternoon free. Another phone call—and a favour owed—meant that she was well on the way to phase one of her plan to save her marriage. She banished the little 'what if?' to the back of her mind. There would be no what ifs. She and Oliver were going to make it. Full stop.

'Are you sure about this, Rachel?' Yvonne asked. 'I mean, it's a big change.'

'I'm sure,' Rachel said.

'Your hair's been mid-length for ages.'

'It's time for a change.' No more scrunchies. She wanted *glamour*.

'It's going to come as a shock. Short and a different colour,' Yvonne warned. 'You'll look in the mirror and howl.'

'Honestly, Yvonne, it's what I want. You know when you get into a rut and you've looked the same for years, and maybe you've grown out of the style?'

'All right.' Yvonne looked thoughtful. 'But I don't think red hair's going to be you.'

With mousy hair, the other option was blonde. 'I don't want to go blonde.' Rachel definitely didn't want to make herself into a carbon copy of Caroline. She wanted *different*.

'How about a compromise? A few copper highlights mixed with a few golden ones. It'll take a bit longer, but I think the results will be worth it.'

'I'm in your hands. Just make me look…' Rachel sighed. 'Well. As if I've made an effort.'

'Is it your wedding anniversary or something?'

Something. Like my husband's having an affair, and I want to remind him what he's missing. 'Let's just say I'm having a bad hair day,' Rachel said lightly.

Two hours later, Yvonne stepped aside and let Rachel see herself in the mirror.

'Wow,' Rachel said softly.

'Like it?'

Rachel nodded. Her new look was going to knock Oliver's socks off. All she needed now was a new dress, some new make-up…and for Ginny to babysit for her tomorrow night. Oliver wasn't going to know what had hit him.

'Hello, love.' Rachel smiled at Oliver when he walked in. 'Coffee?'

'Thanks.' He frowned. Something was different about Rachel. He couldn't quite put his finger on it, but something was different. Or maybe it was just the fact that her pre-menstrual bad mood had passed. At least she was smiling at him for once. 'How are you feeling?'

'Me?'

'Caroline said you'd cancelled lunch because you weren't well.'

'Oh.' She looked slightly taken aback, and Oliver felt his pulse speed up.

Was Rachel lying to him? But why? She hadn't been home, that was for sure, because he'd called her to see how she was feeling and ask if she wanted him to bring anything home. She hadn't answered the phone. At the time he'd thought maybe she just hadn't heard the phone—maybe she'd gone to lie down and had switched the phone off upstairs. Now he wasn't so sure. But if she hadn't been at home, where had she gone instead?

'I had a headache. Probably because it's been hot today. I took a couple of paracetamol.'

Maybe he'd been right the first time and she'd switched the phone off upstairs and had a nap. Oliver felt himself relax again.

'I thought it might be nice to go out tomorrow night.'

'Hmm?'

'Dinner. You and me. And then maybe Saturday afternoon we can have some family time—take the kids to the beach or something. We haven't been to the seaside for ages.'

True. Because parking at the beach was a nightmare in the summer months, particularly at weekends. 'If it's as hot as it was today, it'll be crowded and we'll never get a parking space,' he grumbled.

'Of course we will. A paddle, a sandcastle, an ice cream and then fish and chips. What do you say?'

If he said no, he'd look churlish. And she was right—they hadn't taken the children to the beach for a while. Maybe this was what they needed, some family time. Maybe then Rachel would relax, and the strain between them would dissolve. 'OK.'

'Great. Ginny said she'll babysit for us tomorrow night.'

She'd already organised it, without checking with him first? Then again, at least she was showing interest in him. 'Have you booked somewhere?'

'No, but I will.' She handed him a mug of coffee and smiled at him. 'If I book a table for eight, that'll give you time to see Friday's last-minute panic appointments first.'

Her eyes were sparkling—he hadn't seen Rachel look like this in years. Not since very early on in their marriage, he thought. Definitely in the days pre-kids. So what had changed overnight?

Then his stomach felt as if it had dropped to the floor. Had someone else put the sparkle in her eyes?

No, of course not. He was just being paranoid. Worried that he'd lose her and someone else would snap her up before he realised what had happened. And she was right. Dinner out would be good for them.

So far, so good, Rachel thought the following evening. OK, so Oliver hadn't actually noticed that she'd had her hair done, and it hurt. Even the children had commented that her hair was a different colour and much shorter, and people had noticed at the surgery. But she shoved her disappointment aside. She knew it wasn't the kind of thing that Oliver, being a typical man, would notice, so she wasn't going to make a big deal out of it. At least he'd agreed to spend some time with her. That was the most important thing.

He'd actually called her from the surgery to say that he was on his way home. Their babysitter would be here any moment now. And Rachel had dressed to kill, in a little black dress she hadn't worn for months and the garnet-and-silver earrings her sister had bought her for her birthday. Tonight she was going to vamp her husband—to the point where he'd forget all about Caroline Prentiss.

'You look, uh, nice,' Oliver said when he walked in the

door and saw Rachel on the sofa, both children cuddled up to her as she read them an adventure story.

'Thank you.' She smiled at him. 'Ginny's going to be here in a minute, so you'd better have a shower and change.' She deliberately uncrossed and crossed her legs, so Oliver would notice that her dress definitely didn't reach her knees—and she was wearing lace-topped hold-up stockings.

She was rewarded with a bloom of colour across his cheekbones.

Good. So at least he still fancied her. She could build on that.

'I thought we could have a glass of wine, too.' They weren't going to get roaringly drunk, just have a couple of glasses, enough to relax them but also enough to put them both over the limit for driving. Champagne, maybe. Something to help her put the fizz back into their marriage and wipe Caroline from his mind.

'I'd better stick to just one. Just in case we get called home.'

Just in case he got called out to a patient, more like, Rachel thought, suppressing a sigh. OK. She'd stick a bottle of champagne in the fridge for when they got back. 'Right.'

She could see him looking at her legs, and hid a smile. Oliver always had been a leg man. And she was planning to wear very high heels tonight instead of the sensible flat shoes she usually wore. Tonight Oliver wasn't going to think about anything except his wife.

'I'll, um, have a shower.' He was still looking at her legs.

'See you in five minutes?'

Ginny was already there when Oliver came downstairs.

'Have a nice time and don't worry about a thing. I've got your mobile phone numbers and the restaurant number in case of emergency, but there won't *be* an emergency,' Ginny said firmly. 'Now, off you go.'

'Thanks, Ginny,' Oliver said, kissing her cheek.

'You're a star,' Rachel added. 'Now, you two, behave—you do exactly what Ginny tells you and you go to bed when she tells you, OK?'

'We will,' Robin and Sophie promised together.

Rachel smiled. If the children went to bed late tonight, they'd wake up late tomorrow. Which meant she'd get an early-morning cuddle with Oliver. A cuddle that might turn into more than just a cuddle. Her pulse beat hard with anticipation as Oliver opened the front door for her. She deliberately walked the way she'd seen models moving on the catwalk, one foot straight in front of the other to make her hips wiggle. And when Oliver opened the passenger door for her and his hand brushed over her bottom, her pulse speeded up another notch. It was working. Everything was going to be all right.

They'd chosen their food, Rachel had drunk a glass of wine perhaps a little too quickly, and she was just about to slip off one shoe and caress Oliver's ankle with her toes when she saw him grimace.

'What?'

He retrieved the mobile phone from his pocket. He'd obviously switched it to silent vibrate mode.

'Home?' she asked, worried.

He shook his head. 'Rach, I'm on call. I can't ignore this.'

Why the hell hadn't he asked someone else to cover him for this evening? Just *one* evening, that's all she'd wanted. The disappointment must have shown on her face because he actually looked shamefaced, but he still answered the call.

'I have to go,' he said when he'd switched the phone off again. 'It's Niamh Brady—she's having a severe asthma attack and her mum's panicking.'

'Wouldn't she be better going straight to the emergency department?' Rachel asked.

'Dervla can't drive and Mick's working away.'

'Then an ambulance. They'll have a nebuliser.'

'I've already told her to call the ambulance. But we don't know how long they'll take to get there. I'm nearer. I said I'd go.' His eyes beseeched her to understand that he was a doctor and he had to put his patients first. But Rachel saw it another way. Although there were alternatives, Oliver would always put his patients first. Before his own family, before his marriage, before everything.

Sometimes Rachel wished he'd never, ever become a GP. At least when he'd reached a certain level as a hospital doctor, he wouldn't have been on call every single night. 'I'll come with you.'

'You don't have to.'

He was hardly going to come back here to finish his meal when he'd seen his patient. For a start, he had no idea how long he'd be. If he ended up going to hospital with the Bradys, he could be hours. And Rachel had no intention of waiting on her own in the restaurant and being aware of the pitying looks from other diners. It was either go home alone or go with him. 'Oliver, we're not going to eat now so I might as well come with you. And you know how scary acute asthma attacks can be. If Niamh's really bad, Dervla's going to be panicking. I can calm her down and explain what's going on while you're helping Niamh—or we can do it the other way round.'

'You've been drinking.'

'One glass.' On an empty stomach. 'OK, you help Niamh. Go and get the car while I settle up and explain to the waiter.'

'I'll make it up to you,' Oliver said.

Yeah, right, Rachel thought. She had a nasty feeling that Oliver was secretly relieved he didn't have to spend time with her on his own. So maybe her don't-rock-the-boat approach wasn't the right one. On the way home from seeing Niamh, maybe it would be time to confront Oliver about Caroline and find out what he was planning to do.

Make or break.

# CHAPTER ELEVEN

'THIS isn't how I planned tonight,' Oliver said as Rachel climbed into the passenger seat.

'Me neither.'

'It was supposed to be just you and me tonight. Dinner.' He changed gear, then rested his hand on her knee. 'And you look gorgeous.' She looked stunning. There was something different about her but he couldn't work out what it was, and he didn't want to upset her by asking. Hell. Most of the time nowadays he got it wrong, and the last thing they needed was more distance between them. 'I was going to rush you through dinner anyway—but not for work. I was going to sneak you off somewhere.' He swallowed. 'I wanted to make love to you under the stars.' Something they hadn't done since the children were born. He'd wanted to recapture some of the magic, the sparkle of their early years together, when they'd walked hand in hand along the beach in the moonlight. And then they'd have gone home and rediscovered each other, made love until the silly hours of the morning.

Rachel said nothing, and he sighed inwardly. What had he expected—a 'we still can'? The call-out had completely broken the mood. And when he snatched a glance at her face, her expression said it all for her. *If you'd used a call-out service, everything would have gone as planned.*

But instead he'd taken a gamble that he wouldn't be called out. A gamble that he'd lost. Please, please, don't let it have cost him his marriage. He bit his lip. 'Rach. Talk to me.'

She pushed his hand off her knee. 'Let's just get to Dervla's.'

Her voice sounded very, very tight. As if she were a wound-up spring. One wrong touch could trigger something nasty. If he pushed her now, they'd have an almighty row—a row that would widen the gulf between them even more. He could tell she was on the verge of giving him an ultimatum, telling him to choose between his job and his family. But how could he choose? Being a doctor: that was who he was. Why couldn't he be a doctor *and* a husband and father at the same time?

Caroline's voice echoed in his head. *You need to get your priorities sorted out.*

He wanted Rachel and the kids to come first. But if he used a locum call-out service for evenings and weekends, he'd be flying in the face of everything his father had done. *Doctors never desert their patients.* It was how he'd been brought up. Years and years and years of conditioning. He could hear his father saying it even now. His mother had always accepted it. Why couldn't Rachel accept it, too?

'I'd better check everything's OK at home,' she said, taking her mobile phone from her handbag. A few moments later she gave a worried murmur. 'Ginny's not answering.'

'She's probably reading Sophie a story. You know what Sophie's like if you try to stop reading in the middle of a story.'

'Yes. I've read enough of them to her.'

He could hear the subtext very clearly: *unlike you.* But before he could think up a suitable retort, they were at Dervla's house. Time to put their patient first.

'How is she?' Oliver asked when Dervla answered the door.

Dervla was shaking. 'She can't breathe. I'm so scared she's going to die!'

'No, she's not. It's an asthma attack—a bad one, but we

can get her through it and help her breathe normally again,' Rachel soothed her. 'Niamh's got through them in the past and she'll get through them again.'

'Have you been getting her to take her inhaler over the last five minutes?' Oliver asked. The inhaler contained bronchodilator drugs, which would reduce inflammation in Niamh's airways and open them up again so she could breathe more easily.

Dervla nodded.

'Is it helping?'

She shook her head helplessly. 'Not really.'

'OK. Did they say how long the ambulance would take?' he asked.

'I don't know. I just don't want my baby to die!' Dervla burst out.

Rachel squeezed her shoulders. 'Try not to worry, Dervla. We're here to help her.'

'I'll take a look at her and see if I can make her more comfortable while we're waiting for the ambulance,' Oliver said.

Dervla led them through to the sitting room, where eight-year-old Niamh was sitting on the sofa, wheezing and gasping for breath.

'OK, Niamh, we'll have you breathing more easily in a minute,' Oliver reassured the little girl. 'I'm just going to do a couple of quick checks to see how you're doing, OK?'

She nodded.

Her pulse was rapid, at 140 beats a minute. A quick question showed Oliver that she couldn't complete a sentence in one breath, and six seconds of counting her breaths showed him that she was breathing way too fast at fifty breaths a minute. He knew he wouldn't even need to do a PEF or peak expiratory flow test, measuring how much air she breathed out compared to what she should be able to breathe out for her height. From the look of her, it was very likely to be less than half her normal flow.

Please, don't let her have a silent chest, he prayed as he took out his stethoscope. A 'silent chest' was where air entry to the lungs was reduced so much he wouldn't be able to hear her breathing.

His prayers were answered. So it hadn't got to the stage where it was life-threatening, he thought with relief. 'Good girl, Niamh. You're doing really well. Let me see you take another puff of your inhaler,' he said.

She struggled to breathe it in, but her technique was good, he noted. So the attack probably hadn't been caused by poor management of her asthma. 'As soon as the ambulance comes, they'll give you a mask with some oxygen to help you breathe,' he said. 'I'm going to give you a tablet which will help.'

Before he could even reach for his bag, Rachel was silently handing him the prednisolone. He squeezed her fingers, mouthing his thanks. They were a good team—always had been, he thought. Clearly Rachel had been watching him and had guessed exactly what he'd been doing. Hopefully the prednisolone would kick in by the time the ambulance arrived—otherwise, he'd need to give Niamh a hydrocortisone injection, and suggest the paramedics give her ipratropium bromide through the nebuliser on the way to the hospital.

'Dervla, do you have any idea what triggered this? Did you do anything unusual today?' Rachel asked, going back to sit beside Dervla and taking her hand.

She shook her head. 'The only thing I can think of is that I was cutting down the weeds at the bottom of the garden.'

'Could be weed pollen,' Rachel said.

Dervla sucked in some air. 'It's my fault.'

'Not if you didn't know that weed pollen was a trigger,' Rachel said comfortingly.

Dervla looked at her. 'I've just realised—you're all dressed up. I've called you both away from—'

'Just dinner. No special occasion,' Oliver cut in. 'So don't worry about it. We're GPs. That's what we're here for, and we're used to it.' He didn't dare look at Rachel's face.

'I'm sorry I spoiled it for you,' Dervla said. 'I just, well, panicked.'

'Any mum does. You should see me when Rob or Soph bang their head. I always think of the worst-case scenario,' Rachel said, swallowing her disappointment and trying to sound light and cheery. *No special occasion.* Just trying to get their marriage back on the rails. And, in the scheme of things, that wasn't so important to Oliver, was it?

Before Oliver could say anything else, Rachel's mobile shrilled.

'That's my babysitter,' she said as she glanced at the screen. Oliver had been right: Ginny had been reading a story to Sophie, ignored the phone, and was now returning Rachel's call to reassure her that all was well. 'Hi, Ginny.'

'Rach. I'm sorry to ring you—I know you wanted a special night out—but Rob's not well.'

'Rob?' Rachel's heart missed a beat.

'He's been saying he has a bit of a tummyache, and he's just started throwing up.'

Which meant throwing up a lot. Ginny wasn't the sort who'd be fazed by a child who'd eaten too much chocolate and had brought it back up, Rachel knew. This was serious stuff.

Vomiting and abdominal pains. It could be any number of things. 'Does it look as if he's throwing up coffee grounds?' she asked, her fingers tightening around the phone.

'No.'

She almost sagged in relief. At least, then, there was no

gastric bleeding: 'coffee grounds' was a sign of internal bleeding.

But it could still be something like appendicitis—the condition was more common in the very young and the very old, and the complications could be nasty. 'I'm on my way,' she said. She switched the phone off. 'Oliver, that was Ginny. Rob's ill. I'm sorry, Dervla, I would wait for the ambulance with you, but—'

'If your little boy's ill, you need to be there with him. I'll be all right,' Dervla said. 'I hope it's nothing serious.'

'Me, too.' Rachel dug her nails into her palms, willing herself to keep calm. 'Oliver, I'll take the car. You get a taxi.'

He stared at her in shock. 'You can't take the car. You're over the limit.'

'I only had one glass of wine.'

'Yes, and it was on an empty stomach. It's not worth taking the risk—if you're breathalysed, it'll be an instant ban!'

'Oliver, Rob's got abdominal pains and he's vomiting.' She stared at him in disbelief. Their child was ill, and he was quibbling about the car? 'Look, if you won't let me drive, you'll have to go instead. I'll get a taxi home when I've seen Dervla off in the ambulance.'

Dervla started to cry. 'I'm so sorry. If only I could drive, I wouldn't have had to call you out. I could have taken Niamh to hospital myself.'

'No, you couldn't,' Rachel said gently. 'She'd need you to comfort her on the way. It's fine, really. Despite what my husband says, I'm very far from being drunk and I'd never, ever put a child at risk. Niamh's safe with me. Oliver will go to Rob.'

'I'll see you later,' Oliver said, his face a tight mask.

If you want a fight, Rachel thought grimly, then you can

have one. The second after I get home and find out how my baby is. Right at that moment, she could cheerfully have throttled him.

When Oliver walked into the house, Ginny was mopping Robin up again and changing him into another pair of trousers. 'I've put the washing machine on with the last two sets of sheets and pyjamas,' she said quietly. 'I thought Rachel was coming?'

'She'd had a glass of wine—she couldn't really risk driving.'

'I feel awful about spoiling your special night out. I know Rachel really wanted you to have some proper time together as a couple,' Ginny said with a rueful smile.

It took a second or two for her words to sink in, then the full impact hit him. Rachel had obviously been discussing their marriage problems with their next-door neighbour, the fact that they rarely spent time together on their own. Oliver ignored the fact that he'd done exactly the same with Caroline. He was just conscious of a wave of resentment and anger that Rachel had talked about his private life with other people and hadn't bothered discussing it properly with him.

'I'd better check Robin,' he said, trying to keep his anger under wraps, and quickly assessed his son. Robin definitely had a temperature. Not spiking a fever, but enough to show he wasn't well. His face was pale and his eyes looked huge. 'Can you tell me where it hurts, sweetheart?' Oliver asked gently.

'My tummy.' Robin rubbed his stomach. 'All over.'

'Has it hurt in the same place all the time?'

'Yes.'

'What sort of pain is it? A pushing pain or a poking pain?'

'A poking pain.'

Appendicitis started with central colicky pain, vomiting,

then a shift of pain to the lower right-hand side of the abdomen. With appendicitis, if you pressed on the left iliac fossa, it sometimes caused pain on the right—known as Rovsing's sign. Oliver tested his theory and Robin winced. 'It hurts, Daddy,' he said, his bottom lip wobbling.

Hell, hell, hell. A positive Rovsing's sign. 'OK, son. I know it hurts, but can you be brave for Daddy?'

Robin nodded, close to tears.

'That's my boy.' He kissed Robin's forehead, and looked at Ginny. 'I'm sorry to ask you this, but could you stay with Sophie, please? Rob might have appendicitis and I don't want to take any chances. I need to get him to hospital.'

'Do you want me to call the ambulance?'

Oliver shook his head. 'Thanks, but it'll be quicker to take him in myself.' He carried Robin down the stairs. 'Daddy's driving you to hospital, darling. We'll meet Mummy there. Don't cry, darling. We'll make you feel better soon.' He paused at the doorway. 'Thanks, Ginny. We owe you one.'

'No problem. Look, I'll take Sophie back to mine—she won't wake up, and you won't have to worry about how long you and Rachel are at the hospital. I'll keep her fed and entertained until you're ready to collect her. I've got your spare key so you don't have to worry—I'll lock up behind me.'

'You're wonderful,' Oliver said. 'I don't know how we can ever thank you.'

'I'll tell you next time Ben's away on a course and there's a spider in my living room,' she said with a smile. 'Take care. Give me a ring and let me know how Rob is, will you? It doesn't matter how late.'

'Of course.' Oliver strapped Robin into the passenger seat and rang Rachel on his mobile at the same time. 'Rachel? It's me. I've checked Robin and I think he might have appendicitis—you know how hard it is to diagnose. I don't want to take any chances so I'm driving him to hospital. Ginny's taking Sophie back to hers. Go in the ambulance with Niamh and Dervla, and I'll meet you in the emergency department, OK?' Before Rachel had a chance to say anything, he'd cut the connection, thrown his phone into the passenger footwell and was driving his son to hospital.

Rachel kept assessing Niamh as methodically and efficiently as Oliver would have done, but part of her mind was screaming to the ambulance to hurry up and get them all to hospital.

'Is your little boy going to be all right?' Dervla asked.

Rachel made an effort to keep her voice calm. 'Oliver thinks it might be appendicitis.'

'I'm so sorry. You must want to be with him, and…' Dervla shook her head, fighting back tears.

'Not a problem. Oliver's with him.'

'It's not the same. When it's your child, you want to be there.'

Rachel nodded. 'But I'll be with him soon enough.' Just when she was about to consider giving Niamh hydrocortisone, the ambulance arrived.

The paramedics put the little girl straight onto oxygen and attached a pulse oximeter to her finger. 'Her sats are eighty-seven on full oxygen. We'll need to admit her,' the first paramedic said, reading off the machine.

'But she's going to be all right?' Dervla asked.

'She'll be fine. She'll probably need to stay in hospital overnight, and they'll give her drugs through a nebuliser to help open up her airways again,' Rachel explained.

'Would you like to come with us, Mrs Brady?' the paramedic asked.

'Can I come, too?' Rachel asked. 'Apart from being Niamh's GP, my son's just been taken to the emergency department—possible appendicitis.'

'Of course,' the paramedic said.

The nearer they got to the hospital, the harder Rachel found it to concentrate, but she forced herself to stay calm and kept reassuring Dervla about Niamh's condition.

'She's in the best place, here,' she told Dervla when they reached the hospital and followed the trolley through to the emergency department. 'I'll ring you tomorrow and see how she is.'

'Thank you. And I hope your little boy's all right,' Dervla said.

'Thanks.' Rachel squeezed her hand, then rushed through to the reception desk and asked about Robin. She was directed into one of the cubicles. When she went in, Rob was lying on the bed, looking pale and in pain, and Oliver was standing beside him, holding one hand and stroking his forehead. He was talking in a low voice, clearly soothing their little boy.

'Mummy,' Robin said weakly, trying to smile.

'Hello, handsome.' She gave him a kiss. 'How are you feeling?'

'My tummy hurts.'

'Oh, darling. We'll make you feel better soon, I promise,' she said, taking his free hand and holding it tightly.

'We're not a hundred per cent sure it's his appendix. The PR exam—' a rectal examination '—didn't reveal any tenderness high to the right.'

'That still doesn't rule out appendicitis,' Rachel said.

'They've taken a urine sample and given him some painkillers,' Oliver told her. 'The paediatric registrar's on his way.'

'Right.' She swallowed hard. Stupid. She knew they were in the right place to get help for Rob. But there were so many things it could be, and the wait for test results gave them time to think about what it might be, to drag the scariest and rarest conditions from their memories. She pulled herself together. Just. Oliver had stepped into her shoes briefly, and she'd stepped into his, so he'd be expecting an update on their patient. 'I was about to give Niamh hydrocortisone when the ambulance arrived. Niamh's sats were low, even on oxygen. I told Dervla I'd ring her tomorrow for an update.'

'Right.'

There was a flicker of anger in his eyes, Rachel noted. Surely he hadn't expected her to stay in the emergency department with Niamh and Dervla when their own child was ill? He'd even said to her that he'd meet her there! Before she had the chance to ask him just what his problem was, the registrar arrived. They stepped out of the cubicle to give him space.

'What was that look for?' Rachel demanded in a cross whisper.

'What look?' He spoke at the same reduced volume, clearly not wanting to draw attention to them but, like Rachel, unable to keep his feelings to himself.

'Don't tell me you expected me to stay with a patient instead of being with my son. And don't you dare tell me *you* would have stayed with her, not with Rob here ill and needing you.'

'It's not that,' he said tightly.

'Then what?'

'If you must know, I'm not very happy that you're telling other people we're in a rocky patch.'

'What? Who?'

'Ginny. It's obvious you've talked it over with her. Who else? Your mum? Your sister?'

She stared at him in disbelief. 'Well, you sure as hell weren't talking to me. Every time I tried, you retreated into your office or you got called out. What was I supposed to do? Be like you and bottle things up and pretend nothing's wrong and I'm a happy little bunny?'

'It's our *private* life. I don't want the whole village discussing us!'

'The way you're carrying on, they'll be talking about us soon enough,' she snarled. How many people had already noticed him sneaking around with Caroline? How many people were already pitying her behind her back? 'Anyway, I didn't discuss anything with Ginny. She's obviously worked it out for herself.'

'And what's that supposed to mean?'

'You're hardly ever there, Oliver. When you are, you're never outside with me and the kids—you're stuck in your office, and even the kids talk about Daddy being 'busy' all the time. It doesn't take a huge leap of the imagination to work out what that means, does it?' Worry about Rob made her temper flare. If he could nitpick at a time like this, then just maybe their marriage wasn't worth saving. 'It's up to you if you want to stay or go, but we can't go on like this.'

'What do you mean, stay or go?'

'What I said. I'm not prepared to play second fiddle any more.'

Oliver stared at Rachel in shock. Was she saying that if he didn't get out-of-hours cover, she'd leave him? 'Are you giving me an ultimatum?'

'Just think about it. Think about what you're doing. Think about what you're throwing away.'

This wasn't fair. If people needed him, he had to be there. Why couldn't she understand that? 'Don't ask me to choose. I can't do that.'

She looked anguished. 'Then where do we go from here?'

'I don't know,' he said. 'Right now, I just don't know.'

# CHAPTER TWELVE

IT WAS another three hours before the doctors decided that Robin didn't have appendicitis after all: it was a urinary tract infection. 'We've done a full blood count, checked his Us and Es and blood glucose. They're all normal, but there were signs of proteinuria—' protein in Robin's urine '—so we're pretty sure it's a UTI and we'll give him a five-day course of amoxycillin,' the registrar said.

'A urinary tract infection.' Rachel let out a sigh of relief. 'Once I knew he wasn't vomiting blood, my first thought was appendicitis.'

'Rovsing's sign was positive,' Oliver added. 'I started thinking peritonitis.'

'No, but when we get the MSU results, I might want to book him in for an ultrasound scan and renal tests,' the registrar said.

The scan and renal tests would check for possible damage to Robin's kidneys, and whether he had a condition known as vesicoureteric reflux, where the urine travelled back up the ureter. The tests were common policy after a first urinary tract infection.

'So we can take him home now?' Rachel asked.

'His prescription's back from Pharmacy so, yes, you can. But make sure you give him plenty to drink,' the registrar warned.

'Plus, make sure when he goes to the loo, he voids his bladder fully and his underwear isn't too tight,' Oliver added.

The registrar grinned. 'That's the upside of having medics as the patient's parents: I don't have to go into the full spiel.

You know the drill about antibiotics and at least you'll stick to it.'

'The downside is that we know too much and we'll panic that it's something really, really rare and drive you bananas with questions,' Rachel said wryly.

'Something like that.' He ruffled Robin's hair. 'Right, young man. You can go home and get some sleep. And maybe let your mum and dad get some sleep, too.'

'I'll ring Ginny and let her know what's going on,' Rachel said as Oliver carried Robin through the car park. When she'd finished the call, she informed him, 'Ginny's keeping Sophie overnight and she'll bring her back in the morning. And I think you should sleep in the spare room tonight.'

'Why?' Because he wouldn't give up his ideal of treating patients like people instead of numbers?

'In case Rob needs me in the night. It's easier if he's in with me—then we won't disturb you,' Rachel said, climbing into the back seat with her son.

'Right.' He could see the logic behind that. But he still had the feeling that she had another reason, too. That she didn't want him in her bed any more. 'Um, I'd better sort out a locum for you, for Monday at least.' He glanced in the rear-view mirror and decided not to suggest Caroline by name. For some reason Rachel didn't seem to like Cally very much. Strange, because he'd thought they'd get on well.

'Do that,' she said, sounding as if she didn't care any more.

They drove home in near silence. Robin was asleep by the time Oliver parked, so he carried his son upstairs.

'I'll see you in the morning,' Rachel said.

Hell. He couldn't let things fester like this overnight. 'Rach. You do know I love you, don't you?' he asked.

She said nothing, just looked at him. And her eyes were filled with doubt.

'I've loved you since the moment I first set eyes on you,' he said softly.

But if she remembered their first meeting, it obviously didn't mean the same to her because as he spoke, her face grew more and more set. Obviously loving her wasn't enough. And he noted that she didn't say it back, didn't tell him that *she* loved *him*. So did that mean she'd fallen out of love with him, that his love wasn't enough for her any more?

Not wanting to face the idea that his marriage was speeding further and further towards meltdown, he sighed and headed for the spare room.

How could he? Rachel thought in anguish as she lay awake beside her sleeping son. How *could* he have used those words to her—the same words his mistress had used to him? She bit her lip. Oliver hadn't been like this when she'd first met him, or when she'd married him, or even when they'd first had the children. So when had he become such a smooth liar? Why hadn't she noticed it had been more than just the practice driving them apart?

And why couldn't she picture a happy ending for them?

Robin was much better in a couple of days and, although Oliver had moved back into their bedroom, Rachel had made it very clear she didn't want him to touch her. She hadn't cuddled into him, even in her sleep, and the mornings he'd woken up wrapped round her, she'd wriggled out of his arms in silence. By the middle of the following week, when Rachel was booked to go on a paediatric course, the strain between them almost hummed. They were both very polite and very cautious, knowing that one wrong word could spark off what might be a final row.

On the morning of her course, Rachel was wearing a little black suit—a suit Oliver couldn't remember having seen before. And she was wearing high heels. She didn't look like an approachable family doctor or a mother of two. She looked *glamorous*.

He swallowed back the flash of jealousy. Ridiculous. They'd hit a rough patch, but she wouldn't throw fourteen years of their life away like that. She'd just dressed up a bit for her course and that was all. She was probably looking forward to a full day of being an adult and having grown-up conversations, instead of doing her shift at the surgery and then spending the rest of her time with the kids. She'd had a rough time recently, what with Sophie's chickenpox and Robin's urinary tract infection, and she'd done most of the nursing herself. Because he, of course, had been busy with the surgery, he thought with a stab of guilt.

'You will remember to pick Rob up at three, won't you?' Rachel asked.

'Of course.'

'Then Sophie.'

'Yes.'

'I'm not sure what time I'll be back—it depends on the traffic, and I might go for a drink and a chat with the others after the course. So if you can feed yourself and the kids, I'll make myself a sandwich when I get in,' she said, not meeting his eyes.

'Right.' Did that mean she had a guilty secret? Or just that she couldn't bear to look at him? He didn't know.

'Good. Bye, Rob.' She kissed her son goodbye. 'Have a nice day at school, and be good for Daddy, OK?'

'Yes, Mummy.' Robin held his mother a little too tightly. So he'd noticed she'd withdrawn, too. Oliver sighed inwardly. This situation wasn't good for the kids. But there wasn't a solution. He'd thought and thought and thought, and there just wasn't a win-win solution. One of them would have to back down. For the sake of their patients, it couldn't be him. But for the sake of their marriage…

Oh, hell. Talk about caught between a rock and a hard place. Whatever he did, he'd fail in a huge part of his life. Why couldn't he have both? Why couldn't he have the family he loved and the job he loved?

'Bye, Soph. You have a nice day, too, and be good for Daddy.'

'Yes, Mummy.' Sophie lisped. She, too, hugged her mother tightly. Oliver couldn't remember the last time the children had done that to him. They didn't climb onto his lap to tell him things either, like they did with Rachel.

Had he become a lousy father as well as a lousy husband?

'See you later, Oliver.'

He didn't get the hug and kiss goodbye, he noticed. Not that he'd expected it, with the mood Rachel was in nowadays.

Even though he'd scheduled a later start for surgery that morning, he was still late for work. He'd managed to drop Robin at school with no problems, but Sophie turned decidedly weepy at the idea of him leaving her at nursery. 'No, Daddy, don't go!' She wrapped her arms around his knees and sobbed, wiping her face on his leg. 'No!'

It took him a quarter of an hour to persuade her to make something with play-dough instead of clinging to him with her face pressed into his leg. Even then he had to sneak out while one of the nursery teachers distracted her, and he couldn't shift the feeling that he was a mean, uncaring father who was neglecting his little girl.

'What happened to you?' Caroline asked.

'Sophie didn't want me to leave her at nursery. She got a bit clingy.' Heartbreakingly so. He added cold water to his coffee, cooling it enough to swallow it straight down. Right now, he needed caffeine. 'I never knew Rachel had to go through that every morning.' She'd never said. Then again, he'd never asked.

'How are things?' Caroline asked.

'Still the same.' He sighed. He felt slightly guilty about talking to Caroline about Rachel—particularly as he'd been so angry with Rachel for talking to their neighbour—but it was *different* with Cally. She'd known him for years and she was good at keeping secrets. 'It's stalemate.'

'You know where her course is being held, don't you?'

'Yes.'

'Then go and meet her for lunch.'

He shook his head. 'She won't have time. You know how intensive these one-day courses are. Anyway, I've got to look after the children.'

'She'll make time for you. And if it turns out you're going to be late back, get a babysitter.'

He shrugged. 'How? It's too short notice.'

She raised her eyebrows. 'If you don't want to spend time with your wife, just say so. Don't make feeble excuses.'

'It's not a feeble excuse, and I *do* want to spend time with her.' Oliver glared at her, affronted. 'I just want things to be how they were.'

'That's not going to happen, Oliver. At least, not on its own. The longer you leave things, the bigger the rift between you is going to get.' Caroline rolled her eyes and shook her head in impatience. 'Men. Sometimes you can be *so* stupid. If your normal babysitter can't make it, I'll look after the kids for you.'

'Really?'

'Really.' She smiled. 'It's not as if I'm a total stranger. OK, it means they'll get take-away pizza for dinner tonight, but that won't hurt them, will it?'

Oliver flung his arms round her and hugged her. 'Thanks, Cally.'

'Just sort it out. You know what you have to do. Stop being so stubborn.'

She'd already texted him that message. Several times. Maybe, Oliver thought, it was time he admitted she had a point. Time he admitted that his *wife* had a point. He'd meet Rachel from her course, take her out and lay his heart on the line. Offer to compromise.

He just hoped it wasn't too late.

'I was very impressed with your contributions, particularly in the last session,' Marty, one of the other course delegates, said to Rachel when the whole group was sitting in the hotel bar for a quick drink at lunchtime. 'So you do a lot of paediatric work?'

'I'm responsible for child health in our practice, yes,' Rachel said with a smile. 'I enjoy it.'

'Me, too.' He gave her an appraising look. 'Rachel, I know we've hardly even had a chance to introduce ourselves, but I was wondering if I could take you to dinner tonight, after the course?' His eyes seemed fixed on her mouth—as if he was wondering what it would be like to kiss her. 'I don't normally do this sort of thing. I mean, I don't make a habit of asking women out. But there's something about you. I'd really like to get to know you better.'

Rachel couldn't remember when a man had last looked at her with that kind of interest. Not since before she'd met Oliver. And it was a hell of a boost to her confidence: a man actually found her attractive. Unlike her husband, who used his job as an excuse to keep his distance from her.

For a split second she was tempted to say yes. It would be good to spend an evening with someone who actually *wanted* to spend time with her. Somebody who wasn't going to have half an ear on his mobile phone and would give her his total attention. Somebody who wouldn't have to rush away within a few minutes, full of apologies.

But eight years ago she'd made a promise to love, honour and cherish. An important promise, one she couldn't—*wouldn't*—break. Even if her husband had already broken it.

'I'm sorry, Marty. I'm enormously flattered, but I'm also married. With two small children.'

'You don't look old enough to be married with children.'

She laughed at the blatant line. 'Thank you, Marty, but we both know I'm a qualified GP. My son's six, so you can work out just how old that has to make me.'

'You can't blame a man for trying,' he said good-humouredly. 'Especially with a woman as beautiful as you.'

So her new image had worked on a stranger. Why hadn't it worked on Oliver? Why hadn't her husband noticed?

She smiled back at him. 'I'm very flattered. But the answer's still no.'

'Your husband's a very lucky man.'

Rachel almost said, 'Try telling him that.' But that wasn't fair. It wasn't Marty's fault that her husband had fallen out of love with her. And she certainly wasn't going to burden a near-stranger with her problems. So she smiled and turned their discussion back to the course.

Oliver remained in the doorway of the hotel, just watching. He'd guessed that the delegates would be in the bar—it happened with most courses. What he *hadn't* expected was to see his wife talking with another man. Talking animatedly, throwing her head back and laughing, putting her hand on his arm.

Jealousy knifed through him. When had Rachel last been that carefree with him? He couldn't remember the last time she'd flirted with him like that. And here she was, lapping up the other man's attention.

Part of Oliver wanted to storm over there, punch the guy on the nose and tell him to keep away from his wife. The more sensible part of him knew that if he did cause a scene like that, Rachel wouldn't be impressed by his macho display. She'd be embarrassed, ashamed and probably very sarcastic to him. He wouldn't have a hope in hell of sorting things out with her tonight.

He probably didn't have a hope anyway. This 'surprise lunch date' really wasn't a good idea. If he turned up in the middle of the delegates, he'd look as if he was some kind of jealous husband who didn't trust his wife. He didn't want to embarrass Rachel like that.

And right now she looked happier than he could remember seeing her look in a long, long time. With a sigh Oliver turned away and headed for his car. He texted Caroline to say she didn't need to pick the kids up, he'd do it himself. And when Rachel arrived home—a surprisingly short time after the course was supposed to finish—he couldn't bring himself to ask her about the mystery man. He tried to sound interested in her course, but all he could think of was how far away she was slipping from him. And he couldn't for the life of him work out how to get her back again.

The following week, Oliver's elder brother left him a message at the surgery to say he'd see him for lunch in the pub. Why did Nigel want to meet him for lunch? Oliver wondered. He hardly ever saw Nigel nowadays, except at family functions. Rachel made no secret of the fact that she didn't like his brother, and their loathing was mutual. Probably because Nigel was used to women falling at his feet, and resented the fact that Rachel didn't adore him, Oliver thought grimly.

'I got you a pint,' Nigel said when Oliver walked into the Red Lion.

Oliver went straight onto red alert. Usually, he was the one buying the pints. Nigel almost never stood his rounds. Which was probably why he could afford to run an expensive sports car and was always nipping off to Madrid or Amsterdam or Venice for the weekend. 'Thanks,' he said cautiously, and sat down.

'So, how are you?' Nigel asked.

'Fine. You?'

'Can't complain. Suzanna keeps my hands full.'

Suzanna was clearly the latest girlfriend—yet another Oliver hadn't met. 'Right,' he said, attempting a smile. Though he could hear Rachel's voice in his ear, irritated rather than amused. *Oh, for goodness' sake, does he have to squeeze imaginary breasts every time he mentions a woman's name?*

'I've ordered us the steak and ale pie,' Nigel said.

Oliver would definitely have preferred a salad. But at least his brother was trying to make an effort. 'Thanks,' he said.

'I saw your Rachel last week,' Nigel continued.

'She didn't say she'd seen you at the surgery.'

Nigel shook his head. 'No, not professionally. Out.'

Out? Rachel hadn't been out—except to her course. At least, to Oliver's knowledge, she hadn't been out anywhere.

'Quite a change of image. You know, the suit and the hairstyle.'

Hairstyle? So *that* was what had been nagging at him. Rachel had had her hair cut. And he hadn't noticed. No wonder she'd been frosty with him.

'The blonde streaks suit her.'

Oliver hadn't noticed anything different about the colour of Rachel's hair either. Another black mark to him. And, he wondered, just what else had he missed?

'You know what they say—new image, new lover.'

Oliver scowled. 'Don't be ridiculous.' Of course Rachel didn't have a new lover. Then he remembered the way she'd been flirting with that guy in the bar last week.

'Just a saying. Keep your hair on,' Nigel mocked.

Oliver forced himself to stay calm. This was what lunch was all about. Nigel was just trying to get a rise out of him—the dull, stolid, boring younger brother who'd fitted into their parents' expectations instead of dumping his responsibilities and pleasing himself about what he did with his life. Sibling rivalry. After thirty-seven years of it, he really ought to know better than to let Nigel's little comments upset him. 'So, tell me about your—Suzanna, is it?'

'Lovely. Blonde and curvy. We're off to Paris at the weekend.'

'Very nice.' Paris. Something he and Rachel had always planned to do, but had never actually made it. Not even on their first anniversary. 'Car going OK?'

'Beauty. You ought to get yourself one, you know.'

'I need something big enough to carry the kids and all their stuff,' Oliver said lightly. A little two-seater convertible was out of the question.

Somehow Oliver made it through lunch with Nigel and back to the practice. He wished he'd made some excuse and not gone because all afternoon he kept hearing Nigel's voice. *You know what they say—new image, new lover.*

It got worse when he saw Nancy Griffiths.

'I feel a bit silly. I should know better at my age. Stood on a nail. Peter pulled it out for me, but he said I ought to come and see you.'

'Absolutely right.' Oliver opened the relevant file. 'Your last anti-tetanus jab was nine years ago, so I'm going to give you a booster to be on the safe side. Can I have a look at your foot?' Gently, he checked for signs of neurovascular injury. There weren't any, so at least he wouldn't have to refer her for an X-ray. 'I need to get this cleaned up, Nancy. It's quite hard to clean wounds in the foot, so what I'll need you to do is to come into the side room with me.' He led her into one of the treatment rooms, then filled a bowl with antiseptic and water. 'I need you to sit here and soak your foot for about fifteen minutes, then I'll come in and put a dressing on for you and give you an anti-tetanus booster. Can I get you a magazine or anything while you're waiting?'

'No, thanks, Dr Bedingfield. But thanks for asking.'

After he'd seen his next patient, he came back to finish treating Nancy.

'I saw your Rachel the other day,' Nancy said as Oliver dried her foot and gently applied a dressing. 'She's got that bloom about her.'

'Bloom?' Oliver asked.

'The bloom of a young woman in love.' She tapped the side of her nose. 'Or a woman who's keeping secret news to herself. Tiny feet, and all that.'

Oliver flushed. 'We're not expecting.'

'I didn't expect you to tell me anything.' She grinned. 'I just noticed, that's all.'

*In love…keeping secret news to herself…* Was he missing something really important here?

Of course not. Rachel would never cheat on him. She wasn't the type. He shook himself and tried to concentrate on his patient. He was at work. He was supposed to be helping his patients, not dragging through the mess of his marriage. Dr Bedingfield first, last and always. Just as his father had taught him.

'I'm going to give you a course of antibiotics as well. Now, even though you might be feeling on top of the world halfway through the course, it's important to finish the course or the wound might get infected.' Antibiotic resistance was a growing problem, made worse by people stopping their tablets as soon as they felt better, rather than finishing the course to make sure all the bugs were eradicated. Even when doctors explained the importance of finishing the course, Oliver knew patients often forgot.

'I need you to keep this dressing dry. Come back and see me in five days. If you notice that the bit around where the nail went in turns red or swollen, or gets more painful, ring me straight away. If you get a fever or see any red streaks on your leg, you need to ring me straight away, too.'

She nodded. 'All right.'

He smiled at her. 'And try to rest it as much as you can.'

She grinned. 'The horses won't muck themselves out, Dr Bedingfield!'

'Delegate. Be bossy,' Oliver said.

'I'm good at that.' She chuckled. 'And you think about what I said.'

Oliver couldn't stop thinking about it for the rest of the afternoon. Two people had tackled him directly and had as good as said that Rachel had a new man. How many others had noticed but were too embarrassed or pitied him too much to tell him? Was he so stupid that he hadn't even noticed her slipping away from him?

By the time he got home his mood had turned really nasty. He answered Rachel in monosyllables—he couldn't trust himself not to snap, and he didn't want to have a blazing row with her in front of the children. It wasn't their fault and he should keep them out of it. But as soon as he heard her come downstairs after putting the children to bed, he stomped out of his office to confront her.

'So when were you going to tell me?' he asked.

Rachel frowned. 'Tell you what?'

'The reason behind the new hair and the new clothes.'

'What are you talking about?'

'The man who's put the smile back into your eyes, if half of Hollybridge is to be believed.'

'What?' She stared at him in what looked like shock.

Did she really think he wouldn't find out in the end? Did she really think she could pull the wool over his eyes for much longer? 'Your lover,' he enunciated coldly.

Her jaw dropped for a moment, and then her gaze hardened. 'I haven't got a lover.'

No?

'*I'm* not the one having an affair.'

Well, *he* certainly wasn't! 'What's that supposed to mean?'

'If this is your way of salving your own guilt, forget it.'

'What are you talking about?'

'You know *exactly* what I'm talking about.'

Was she trying to say that his work was like a mistress? When would she stop nagging him about his job, about who he was? He could feel his mouth tighten as he snapped at her, 'Now you're being ridiculous.'

'Ridiculous? I'm not the one throwing accusations about without a shred of proof!' She folded her arms. 'You're not the man I married, Oliver. If you can accuse me of having an affair—when I've never, ever even *thought* about another man, much less gone to bed with one—then obviously the trust has gone in our marriage. And, without trust, a marriage isn't worth anything.'

As suddenly as it had boiled over, his anger vanished. Fear took its place. A gut-wrenching, numbing fear. As if the floor had suddenly dissolved and he was falling, falling into a bottomless pit.

*Without trust, a marriage isn't worth anything.*

He hadn't trusted her. Was she saying that she didn't trust him any more either? Was she saying that their marriage wasn't worth anything any more—that she wanted out?

He could barely choke the words out. 'What are you trying to tell me, Rachel?'

Her voice dropped to a whisper, as if the words were torn unwillingly from her. 'I'm not sure if I want to be married to you any more.'

## CHAPTER THIRTEEN

'YOU'RE leaving me?' Oliver asked in shock. He'd wanted everything out in the open, yes, but he hadn't expected this. He hadn't expected it to be so easy for Rachel to discard fourteen years of being together. Or was it only easy because she'd been thinking about it for a long time, and he hadn't even noticed anything was wrong?

'Right now,' she said quietly, 'I'm thinking about asking *you* to leave. I'd rather bring up Rob and Sophie on my own than make them live in an atmosphere like this.'

'Like this?' he asked, knowing that he sounded like a demented parrot, repeating her words, but at the same time unable to force out the words he wanted to say. He didn't want her to bring up Rob and Sophie on her own. They were a family. They belonged together, and he didn't want to leave.

'Like this. When we don't talk to each other, don't spend time with each other, don't pull together like a proper family. It's not good for them. It's not good for *any* of us. I've put up with it for way too long, Oliver, and I just can't live like this any more.'

This wasn't happening. This really wasn't happening. Any moment now he was going to wake up and he'd be lying in bed, sweating and staring-eyed after his nightmare, with Rachel in his arms.

Any moment now.

A heartbeat passed.

Then Oliver realised it was all true. That his marriage was on the point of sliding into an abyss. He sucked in some air. 'Rachel, please. I don't want things to be like this between us. I don't want our marriage to be over. Rach, I know things haven't been good lately, but—'

'But nothing, Oliver.' Her eyes were dark with sadness. 'It's time we faced it. It's not working between us. It hasn't worked properly for a long time. Without trust, there's nothing worth saving in our marriage.'

'No. You've got it wrong. I trust you. Of *course* I trust you. You're my wife, the mother of my children.' The woman he loved above all else. He'd walk over burning coals for her. Climb Everest. Swim through shark-infested waters. 'Hell, Rachel.' He tugged a hand through his hair, hoping the minor pain would be enough to clear his head and let him think straight, so he could say the right thing to stop their marriage sliding away. 'I don't know why I said what I did. I don't know… Hell,' he repeated, shaking his head. This was all going so wrong. 'The only thing I do know, right now, is that I love you.'

And he meant it from the depths of his soul. So why did she look as if she didn't believe him?

'I can't believe you accused me of having an affair, when you…when you…' Her words choked off. She was crying. Silently, which made it that much worse. Tears were just leaking out of her eyes as if she couldn't stop them. Hating himself for what he'd done to her, he reached over to pull her into his arms. If he held her—if they held each other—maybe everything would be all right.

'No.' Her voice was breathy between sobs. 'Don't touch me, Oliver. Not right now. I can't bear it.'

'I'm sorry.' Panic was galloping through his veins. How was he going to fix this? Maybe Cally could help. Maybe Cally could explain where he'd gone wrong, what he could do to make it up to Rachel, how he could prove to his wife that he loved her more than anyone in the world. That she was the sunlight in his days. 'Rach.' His mouth felt as if it was full of one of Robin's peanut butter and Marmite sandwiches, as if his tongue was stuck to the roof of his mouth. 'Don't leave me. We can't…' He reached out to her again.

She took a step back. 'I need some space,' she said, her voice shaking. 'And I'd appreciate it if you slept in the spare room tonight.'

She didn't want him to sleep in their bed any more? 'But…' His voice faded. If he pushed her now, said they couldn't leave it like this, he might make things ten times worse. If he gave her an ultimatum, she might ask him to leave. At least this way they'd still be in the same house. He'd be in the spare room, yes, but he wouldn't be on the other side of the village. He'd be near enough to persuade her to give him another chance. To work with him and mend their marriage. 'If that's what you really want,' he said carefully.

She opened her mouth, but nothing came out. Then she gave Oliver a look that chilled him to the bone and walked away.

Burying himself in work didn't help the way it usually did— he couldn't even concentrate on what he was doing. So he switched off his computer and headed upstairs. He paused for a moment outside their bedroom door. Should he go in? Should he tell her he'd made a stupid, *stupid* mistake and he bitterly regretted it, that he didn't know what the hell was happening and he wanted it all to stop, wanted everything to be how it used to be? But then he remembered the way she'd looked at him. She'd told him she needed space. If he pushed her too hard now, it might be the end of everything. Maybe tomorrow, when they'd both had a chance to cool down, he could try again. And this time he wouldn't make such a mess of things.

He sighed, had a quick shower, then went into the spare room. Wishing, every second, that his wife was back in his arms. And wondering if it was already too late.

\*     \*     \*

Rachel heard Oliver's footsteps outside the door. Heard him stop. Part of her desperately wanted him to come into their room, take her in his arms and tell her that everything was going to be all right, that they'd make it through all this mess together. The other part of her knew that this was a turning point. That this was the beginning…of what? The end? Or a change for the better? Right now she wasn't sure which. She wasn't even sure what she wanted any more. As she'd told Oliver, without trust their marriage was nothing but an empty shell. And if he could believe that she was having an affair—if he'd somehow twisted things round in his mind to give himself an excuse for his affair with Caroline—then he wasn't the man she'd married. He wasn't the man she'd sworn to love until death did them part.

Tears leaked down her face. She squeezed her eyelids shut, but it didn't stop her crying silently, weeping for what she'd lost and feeling colder and lonelier than she'd ever been in her life before.

The next morning, her eyes felt as if they'd been sand-blasted and her head was heavy and throbbing from lack of sleep.

'Mummy, your eyes are all red,' Robin said. 'And they're puffy.'

'I'm all right,' Rachel lied. She took a paracetamol. 'It's just an allergy.'

'Oh. All right,' Robin said.

'You look terrible,' Oliver murmured to her. 'Don't come in to work today.'

Why? So he could have his mistress nearby again as Rachel's locum? Or because he didn't want anyone at the surgery to realise Rachel had spent the whole night crying, and then guess why—bring his dirty little secret out into the open? She lifted her chin. Tough. She wasn't going to cover for him. 'I'll be perfectly all right,' she informed him tightly, and refused to meet his eyes. She didn't want to talk to him, not now. Not in front of the children. She didn't want them to see their parents' marriage ending right in front of their eyes.

She wore dark glasses when she dropped the children off, so at least nobody at school or nursery made a comment about her eyes. But she couldn't hide it at the surgery.

'Rachel, you poor thing! Are you sure you're well enough to be here?' Rita asked, fussing over her.

'I'm fine. Hay-fever season,' Rachel said, hoping Rita wouldn't call her bluff and remember that Rachel had never suffered from hay fever.

Somehow, she got through the first half of her list. But when she took her coffee-break, Oliver was already in the rest room.

She turned away, muttering, 'I'll come back later.'

'Don't,' Oliver said softly, taking her hand from the door and closing it again. 'Rach, sit down.'

No. She couldn't handle a discussion. Not right now. But she found herself sitting down anyway.

'Coffee.' He handed her a mug.

'Don't be kind to me, Oliver,' she said. She really, really didn't want his pity.

'I'm not being kind. I'm trying to apologise,' he said in a low voice. 'Rachel, I'm so sorry. I should never, ever have said what I did. I wasn't thinking straight yesterday.'

'You can say that again.'

'I'm sorry. I suppose I felt guilty because I hadn't noticed your new image—and I jumped to the wrong conclusion.'

'I did it to get *your* attention, Oliver. You were the only one I ever wanted.' To her horror, her voice was wobbly. She swallowed hard. 'But if you can think that badly of me, without even discussing it with me, then you're not the man I married.'

'I've been an idiot. I don't know—'

But whatever he'd been about to say was cut off by Rita rushing into the room. 'Dr Bedingfield!'

'Yes,' they answered in unison.

'It's Wayne Groves, Lesley's boy. She thought he had the flu, but he's been getting worse so she made him come in—and he's just collapsed. Could you come?'

'Let's take him into my office,' Oliver said. Between them, he and Rachel supported the sixteen-year-old into Oliver's consulting room and sat him on the couch.

'Can you tell us how you've been feeling?' Rachel asked.

'Awful,' Wayne mumbled. 'Head hurts, feel sick. Don't want to eat.'

'He's been complaining of all sorts of aches and pains. I thought it was summer flu or something,' Lesley said, looking anxious. 'He's been off his food, which isn't like him, and he says he feels sick every time he lies down.'

'My eyes hurt,' Wayne said.

Rachel could identify with that. Hers were sore, too.

'He's supposed to be starting a job next week,' Lesley said. 'Just for the summer, till he goes to college in September. But I'm not sending him out to work like this.'

'Be all right, Mum,' Wayne muttered.

Rachel examined him gently. 'There's some bruising on your skin, Wayne.' When she touched his calves, he winced. 'Your legs are sore?' she asked.

He nodded.

'I don't think this is flu.' And she wasn't aware of any flu doing the rounds. 'It could be Weil's disease,' she said. If it was, it was a notifiable disease, meaning that they'd have to tell the public health office—and the lab would want to know where the source was.

'Wayne, have you done anything involving water lately?' Oliver asked.

He nodded. 'Went swimming in the weir after the exams—it was so hot.'

'Did you swallow any of the water?' Rachel asked.

Wayne shrugged. 'Might've done. But the weir's safe. We've always swum in it.' He glanced at his mother. 'I know Mum'd have a fit if I ever swam in dirty water, so that's why we go to the weir.'

'It might not *look* dirty,' Oliver said, 'but if water's draining into the weir from the farmland around it, it might be infected with the *Leptospira* bacterium—probably *Leptospira icterohaemorrhagiae*, which can be pretty nasty.'

Wayne pulled a face. 'My mates went with me and none of them have got it.'

'Yet,' Rachel warned. 'The incubation period is any time from two to twenty-six days. So it depends on how susceptible you are to the infection, the level of infection in the water and whether the bacteria enter your body.'

The teenager worked out what she meant and a look of disgust passed over his face. 'That's *gross*.'

'How long have you been feeling rough, Wayne?' Oliver asked.

'Couple of days.'

'We'll need to get a blood test to the lab to check for the bacteria, and we'll need you to give us a urine sample before you leave. In the meantime, we need to start treating you,' Oliver said. While Rachel did the blood test and gave Wayne a sample bottle for the urine test, Oliver checked Wayne's records to see if the boy was allergic to penicillin. He wasn't. 'OK. We'll give you a week's course of penicillin to start with. And I'd suggest you get your mates to come and see us for some antibiotics, just in case—the earlier we catch it, the better it is.'

Rachel exchanged a glance with him. Hopefully they were treating Wayne early enough. With Weil's disease, some patients went on to develop jaundice, anaemia, renal failure and even cardiac problems. More worryingly, it could be fatal in a small number of cases.

'So is Wayne going to be all right?' Lesley asked.

'Hopefully,' Oliver said. 'It's a notifiable disease, so the public health lot will want to talk to Wayne about the weir.'

'I don't want to get anyone into trouble,' Wayne said.

'You won't get anyone into trouble,' Rachel said gently. 'It'll just help them identify the source so they can clear up the infection and make sure nobody else gets it.'

'You must take the antibiotics regularly, Wayne, and finish the whole course,' Oliver said. 'If you get a stiff neck or a really severe headache, ring us straight away. I want to see you again in a week so I can do some more blood tests to see how you're doing.'

'All right, Dr Bedingfield.'

'Try not to worry, Lesley,' Rachel said gently. 'I know what it's like when your child's ill—you feel helpless, wish you could have it in their stead. We'll ring you as soon as the test results are back, and you can ring us any time if you're worried.' She squeezed Lesley's shoulder.

'Thank you,' Lesley said, her face white with strain, and led her son out of the consulting room.

'Rachel,' Oliver said softly when they were alone.

'I'm late for my list,' she said, and hurried out of the room—knowing that she was being a coward, but unable to face him right at that moment.

When Oliver finished surgery, he checked the appointments screen and discovered that Rachel had already gone.

No surprises there. But hurt bloomed like a bruise inside him. They'd worked together today. Worked *well* together. Didn't that prove anything to her?

He took his wallet from his drawer, planning to start his house calls. But then the catch on his wallet snapped and papers spilled out. Papers, including a photograph of him and Rachel. A very old photograph, taken in a photo booth. They'd been together for six months, and he'd been happier than he could ever remember. Love almost radiated round them like a halo. They were both laughing and Rachel was looking at him as if he was her entire world.

When had she stopped looking at him like that?

He didn't know. But he wanted it back. All of it. He wanted the woman he'd wooed and loved and laughed with. And if it meant disappointing everyone else, then so be it: Rachel was too important for him to lose.

He went to see the practice secretary. 'Prunella, can you do me a favour?' he asked.

'Of course, Dr Bedingfield.'

'Can you reschedule my house calls, please?'

She looked at him as if he'd grown two heads. Hardly surprising. He never, but never, rescheduled patients. He might keep them waiting a little while if a consultation over-ran, but he always worked through to the end of his list. Well, today was different. His marriage couldn't wait. 'Prunella?' he asked gently.

'Er—yes, Dr Bedingfield. Of course.'

'Thank you. And I won't be available for the next hour.'

So what if the village started talking? He didn't care any more. He wanted Rachel back, and he wanted her *now*. Later, he'd give her flowers. He'd give her the moon, if that was what she wanted. Right now he was going to offer her his heart. And he only hoped it wasn't too late.

# CHAPTER FOURTEEN

RACHEL'S face went white and she nearly dropped her mug of coffee when Oliver walked into the kitchen.

'I wasn't expecting you home. Aren't you supposed to be doing house calls?' she asked.

'I've asked Prunella to reschedule them.'

'You've asked…?'

Was it *that* shocking? Did she really feel he put the practice before her every single time? Hell. If he didn't do something now, he had a nasty feeling that their marriage would disintegrate completely. 'We need to talk, Rach,' he said softly. 'And I'd rather we didn't have this conversation in front of the children.'

'Me, too.'

She looked as grim as he felt. Please, God, don't let her ask me to leave for good, he thought desperately. Please, don't let it be too late. He swallowed hard. 'I'm not the best person with words. Not when it comes to something as important as this.'

He saw her grab onto the kitchen table, her fingers tightening against the wood. What was going on in her head? Did she want him to leave or stay?

'I just want you to know—'

The phone shrilled, cutting him off.

'You'd better answer it,' Rachel said dully. 'It's probably a patient.'

Oliver swore. 'Leave it,' he said. 'Let the answering machine take it.'

'But—'

163

'But nothing. I'm sick of interruptions. Every time we try to talk, someone else cuts in. This is too important to leave.'

*Tell her. Tell her how you feel.* The words echoed in his head.

'I love you.'

She blinked at him. 'What?'

'I love you,' Oliver said. 'You mean everything to me.'

'No.' She shook her head. 'Don't lie to me, Oliver. I know the truth.'

Truth? He stared at her in surprise. 'What are you talking about?'

'Caroline Prentiss.'

'What about her?'

'Your mistress.'

'My *what*?' He stared at her, uncomprehending. What the hell did she mean? Just because his elder brother was a womaniser, it didn't mean that *he* was. He shook his head, hardly able to believe that they were having this conversation. 'I've never been unfaithful to you. I never could be. I'm not having an affair with anyone, least of all Caroline.'

She lifted her chin, challenging him. 'Come off it. I heard it all in the playground. You used to go out together, and everyone thought that you'd end up getting married—but then she broke it off and you met me. You married me on the rebound. And the moment she was back, you were all over her like a rash!'

'No, I wasn't.'

'Oliver, I saw that text message she sent you. ''I've loved you since the moment I first set eyes on you. I knew you were the one I wanted to grow old with. That hasn't changed and it never will. I love you.''' Her voice was shaking. 'And, even worse, you actually started to use that line on me!'

He flushed. 'I swear to you, it isn't like that. Anyway, why were you looking at my text messages?'

'Because I thought you were being unfaithful. And I

found proof. When are you going to stop denying that she's your mistress, Oliver?'

'She *isn't* my mistress. And that message wasn't about me.'

'You're not making any sense.'

He dragged a chair out, made her sit down and pulled a chair out for himself next to hers. 'Caroline was my girlfriend when I was a teenager, yes. But she didn't feel the same way about me as I felt about her.'

Rachel scoffed. 'I saw you the night she came over for dinner. You were virtually glued to each other in the hallway. I mean, in our house, with our children asleep upstairs and when you thought I was in the kitchen. How could you?'

'It really isn't what you think.' He raked a hand through his hair. It wasn't his secret to tell. But if he didn't tell Rachel the truth now, he'd lose her for good. If he hadn't already lost her. 'Look, I'm not having an affair with Cally.' He took a deep breath. 'She's gay.'

'What?'

'She's gay. A lesbian. Except she's always kept it very quiet so people in Hollybridge don't know—you can imagine the kind of hassle her parents would get, with her dad being the vicar. All the stuff about sin and that—even nowadays, people would gossip about her and make hurtful remarks and her parents would probably get the brunt of it. Back when we were teenagers, attitudes were even worse. Nobody would have accepted her for who she is.'

'So let me get this straight. You're telling me she wasn't *ever* your girlfriend?'

'Yes. No. It's complicated.' Oliver sighed. 'I *thought* she was my girlfriend, yes, when we were teenagers. We virtually grew up together, with our parents being friends and the fact we both went to the same school. I liked her. And, yes, people said we made a good couple. I asked her out and she said yes. But then one day things… Well. I wanted to make love, she didn't.' He could feel his skin heating. He really didn't feel comfortable, discussing an ex with his wife—discussing making love with another woman—even though it had been years ago. 'Then she started crying, and she told me the truth. How she thought of me as a friend, her best friend, as if I were the brother she didn't have. She didn't feel the same way about me that I felt about her, but it wasn't my fault, it was hers, because she couldn't feel like that about any one male. She preferred women. But she knew it would kill her parents if they found out the truth, so she asked me if I'd still pretend I was her boyfriend, be her cover until she was at Oxford and far enough away from Hollybridge for it not to matter any more.'

'Caroline's a lesbian,' Rachel said slowly.

'Yes.'

'But she doesn't look…' She bit her lip. 'Um. Sorry.'

'She's not butch, no. She's always been very girly. Unlike one of her girlfriends.' He grimaced. 'Sam treated Cally incredibly badly. She was the reason Cally had a breakdown at Oxford. Everyone thought it was because of me, that I'd called it off between us. But I didn't mind taking the flak because I knew she couldn't tell anyone the truth, not even her parents. Nobody else would understand.'

'Why didn't you tell me about her?'

He shrugged. 'I didn't think there was any point. Cally swore she'd never come back to Hollybridge, and then she went to Australia. We lost touch and I didn't think I'd ever see her again. Besides, it wasn't my secret to tell.'

'Couldn't you have trusted me once she came back to Hollybridge?'

'I wanted to. But, as I said, I'd promised her years ago I wouldn't tell anyone.'

'And your loyalty to her was stronger than it was to me.'

'No, it wasn't like that.' He shook his head. 'You come first, Rach.'

'So why are you telling me now?'

'Because I'm scared that if I don't, I'm going to lose you. I'm scared that it might already be too late.'

Rachel still didn't look convinced. 'If she's not in love with you, why did she send you that text?'

He should have guessed that she'd want an explanation. 'You're not going to like this,' he warned.

'What? She's changed her mind about her sexuality?'

'No. I, um, told her we'd been having problems.'

'What? When you'd had a go at me for talking to my sister, and accused me of telling Ginny and half the village?'

'You and I were hardly talking, and I was going slowly insane. I'm not good with words, not when it really matters. I wanted you to know that even though things were bad between us, I really did—*do*—love you. And she came up with the words to help me tell you how I felt.'

'You were going to tell me words that someone else had thought up for you?' Her lip curled in disgust.

He swallowed. 'They might not be my words, but it's exactly how I feel. I told her about when I first met you. That time I saw you in the library, studying. You were concentrating, bent over the desk with your elbow on the table and one hand stuck through your hair. I couldn't see your eyes but I could see your mouth, and all I wanted to do was kiss it.' Just like he wanted to kiss her now. 'I sat opposite you and you looked up. And it just hit me. I didn't even know your name, but I'd fallen in love with you. I wanted to be with you. Have kids with you. Grow old with you. It's how I've always felt about you, Rach, right since that very first moment.' He took his wallet from his back pocket and pulled out the photograph. 'Remember this? I didn't think I'd ever be any happier than this. Well, except on the day you stood next to me to the altar and said, "I do."'

She took the photograph and stared at it thoughtfully. He still couldn't work out what she was thinking, what she was feeling.

Talk to me, Rachel, he pleaded silently. Tell me you love me as much as I love you. That you want to make a go of our marriage.

She looked at him. 'What about Caroline?'

'Cally's my friend. Someone who's known me for years. Someone who's been nagging me even more than you have about the way things are between you and me.' He took a deep breath. 'I thought you'd found someone else.'

'That's ridiculous.'

'Is it? When you did your paediatrics course, I decided to meet you from your course and have lunch with you. Or at least ask you to go out with me that night. Cally said she'd babysit, and I wanted to take you out to dinner. Give us some space to talk. But then I got to the hotel and saw you. You were flirting with a man in the bar.'

'A man in the…?' She chewed her lip. 'Oh, Marty.' She shook her head. 'That didn't mean anything. He was just one of the other delegates. He asked me out. And I admit, I was flattered that a man had paid me some attention—I mean, you didn't even notice that I'd completely changed my hair and I'd started dressing up again instead of being mumsy.'

'I *did* notice. You looked stunning. I just… The way things were between us, I didn't know how to tell you without you taking it the wrong way and having a fight with me.'

'I turned him down, Oliver. I told him that I was married. I never even… Oh, perhaps for a second I thought about saying yes. It felt good, knowing that someone found me attractive. Except he wasn't you.' She put the photograph on the table and twisted her fingers together. 'Is that why you accused me of having an affair?'

'Yes. I didn't know what to think, Rach. First I see you flirting with a stranger, then people in the village hint that you're seeing someone. You know—new man, new image.'

'I was trying to show you that I could be as glamorous as your mistress.'

'I don't have a mistress.'

'I know that now.' She bit her lip. 'I'm sorry I doubted you. I should have known… But I thought you'd fallen out of love with me—that you escaped to the practice rather than spend time with me.'

'No. I thought you'd stopped loving me. You spend all your time with the kids and you never have time for me any more.'

'Oliver, that's crazy. How can you be jealous of your own children? They're *little*. They need me.' When she saw the flash of hurt in his eyes, she added, 'They need you, too.'

Then her heart caught up with her brain. Oliver thought she didn't have room for him any more, since the kids. 'Just because I love them, it doesn't stop me loving you as well,' she said softly. She remembered what his childhood must have been like, trailing in the wake of Nigel and knowing that he was second best, only ever wanted when his elder brother wasn't around. 'Love isn't something you chop up into little bits and once it's shared out there's nothing left. It grows with you as a couple, expands to encompass your children and then their families.' She reached over to take his hands. 'I'm sorry if you felt left out. If you thought we didn't need you, didn't have time for you any more, no wonder you turned to the practice.'

'We've both been stupid,' Oliver said.

'We should have talked,' Rachel agreed. 'I wanted to. But I was so scared you were going to say you didn't want us any more, I ducked the issue.'

'Me, too.' He stroked her face. 'I don't want to fight any more, Rach. I just want you back. I want things to be how they were—when we were happy.' He took the photograph from the table and tucked it back into his wallet. 'You, me and the kids. A proper family.'

'Me, too,' Rachel said. 'But I don't want to go back to how things have been these last few months, when you haven't had time for anything except work and I've spent all my time with the kids.'

'I was trying—'

'To do the impossible,' Rachel said.

'I thought I could keep my father happy by running the practice as he'd always run it. But times change. And the Bedingfield Surgery is going to have to change, too, because I can't do it all.'

'And I'll support you more. Maybe I can get Sophie in for another session at nursery and take some of the burden off you, so we can spend more time together. And maybe we can put aside one evening a week just for us, so we don't lose each other again.'

'An evening that's not interruptible. Ever.' He leaned over to kiss her. 'I love you. And I've been thinking. Everything you've been saying to me…you're right. I'm going to use an on-call service to take over the night and weekend calls, and hire a practice manager to handle the admin side of things.'

'Using an on-call service won't make you any less of a family doctor,' Rachel said. 'You'll still be Dr Bedingfield.'

'But I'll also be a husband and father, and put you and the kids first,' Oliver said. 'I don't want to sit there at their eighteenth birthday parties and realise that they've grown up and I missed every step along the way because I put the practice before my family.'

'They've been missing you, too,' Rachel told him. 'And so have I.'

'It's not going to happen overnight, and we'll still have hiccups,' he warned.

'But we'll work together. Get through the hiccups together. We'll talk about things.'

'From now on, I'm going to tell you every day that I love you. And I mean it, from the bottom of my heart.' He held her close. 'Just tell me you'll forgive me. That we can start again.'

'I don't want to start again.'

He pulled away from her in horror. 'You still want me to leave?'

'I never did want you to leave. But I don't want us to pretend none of this ever happened, Oliver. I want us to remember it. So we never, ever repeat the mistakes again.'

'No more trying to be perfect, trying so hard not to rock the boat that we don't realise there's an iceberg dead ahead,' Oliver said. 'We'll talk properly in future. Starting right now.'

'Sounds good to me.' Rachel curled back into his arms. 'I love you, Oliver.'

'And I love you, too.' He kissed her. 'And tonight I'm not sleeping in the spare room. In fact, we might not be doing that much sleeping.'

'I hope,' Rachel said softly, 'that's a promise.'

'Oh, it is.' His eyes held hers. 'In fact, I'm going to ring Prunella now and ask her to give me another hour.'

'No, you're not—you'll feel too guilty. But tonight you're mine—all *mine*.' She kissed him lightly. 'Go and pick that message up.'

'Sure?'

'Sure. But if you're more than ten minutes, I'll bring your coffee in to you. And I might be tempted to distract you from the phone.'

'Now that's an offer I won't refuse.' He kissed her. 'I love you, Rachel. More than words can tell.'

'And I love you, too.'

# CHAPTER FIFTEEN

SEVEN minutes later, Oliver stumbled back into the kitchen.

'That was my mother. My father's had a stroke. A couple of hours ago.' He stared at her in shock. 'She tried to ring me, but she couldn't get through to the surgery. And when she did get through, I'd left. She couldn't remember my mobile number so she rang here.'

And Oliver hadn't taken the call because he'd been trying to please her, trying to sort out the mess of their marriage.

She could see the guilt in his eyes. The misery. Whatever he did, he lost. If he'd taken the call, it might have been the last thing to push their marriage over the edge. But he'd put his marriage first, and now it might be too late for his father.

'Did you reach her at the hospital?'

He nodded.

Well, of course he had. Stupid question. It didn't take that long to replay an answering-machine message. Rachel added sugar to her husband's coffee—Oliver didn't take sugar, but it was supposed to be good for shock—and pressed the mug into his hands. 'So how is he?'

'Don't know. They're still doing tests. They think it was a cerebral embolism.' An embolism was a clot that formed in one of the blood vessels in the body and travelled up to lodge in the brain—it starved the brain cells of oxygen and led to a stroke.

'I'll drive you to the hospital.' She could see the protest starting to form in his face. *What about the surgery?* 'I'll take your afternoon list, and I'll call in some favours so Rob

172

and Sophie can go to a friend's for tea and I'll pick them up after surgery.'

'I…' He shook his head, clearly too stunned to continue his sentence.

'Just take a swig of that.'

He did, and grimaced. 'Yuck. Too sweet.'

'Good for shock,' she said crisply. 'Get in the car. I'll lock up. You can tell me more on the way there.'

Numbly, he followed her directions.

'Did you mother say how severe it was?'

'Just that his right arm went numb, and then he said he felt a bit funny. Then he started rambling and she couldn't understand what he was saying, but she could see he couldn't swallow properly. She rang the ambulance, and on the way to hospital they told her they thought he'd had a stroke. They're doing tests now.'

She reached over to squeeze Oliver's hand briefly between gear changes. 'He'll be fine, Oliver. Most stroke patients recover.'

'Mmm.' But they both knew the figures. If you survived a stroke, you had a fifty per cent chance of a severe disability, and it could take up to eighteen months to recover.

They were silent for the rest of the drive. Rachel pulled up outside the entrance to the hospital. 'I'll drop you here and go straight to the surgery,' she said. 'Ring me as soon as you know any more. Rita'll put you through, even if I've got a patient with me.'

'But—'

'Your father takes top priority right now,' Rachel cut in gently. 'Everything else goes on hold until we know what the situation is.'

'Thank you.'

Then she realised that his eyelashes were wet and spiky. Oliver, who was always so laid back, who never really showed emotion. The last time she could remember him crying was when Sophie was born, and even then he'd denied that he'd had tears in his eyes.

She reached over and hugged him. 'I'm here for you, Oliver. I love you. And everything's going to be OK, I promise.'

Though the look on Oliver's face said the opposite. She knew how his mind worked: the minute he'd decided to change his father's way of running the practice, his father had had a stroke. And Oliver wouldn't see that as a coincidence. So was their 'new beginning' really the end?

Please, God, let Stuart recover. And let Oliver see that he was doing the right thing, for all of their sakes.

Later that afternoon, the phone on her desk shrilled. 'Rachel? It's me.'

'How's your dad?'

'Holding on. It was a cerebral embolism,' Oliver told her. 'They did an electrocardiogram and he's got atrial fibrillation.' Atrial fibrillation—an irregular heartbeat—became more common as you got older, and increased the risk of stroke by causing blood clots to form in the heart, which could then break off and travel through the arteries to the brain. 'The MRI scan confirmed there was a clot. They've done blood tests and they're going to put him on warfarin.' Warfarin made the blood less 'sticky' and reduced the risk of another blood clot forming in the heart and travelling to the brain. 'His right arm's still a bit weak, but physiotherapy will help with that.'

Rachel knew that communication problems were very common, too—anything from not being able to think of the right word to use in the middle of a sentence through to a complete inability to speak. And if his right arm was affected, it meant that the stroke was on the left side of the brain, which also controlled language and thought. 'How's his speech?'

'A bit slurred. We don't know if his understanding is affected. The speech therapist is coming tomorrow. He's still not swallowing properly.' It was common not to be able to swallow properly for the first week or so after a stroke—that meant there was a risk of food or drink going down the wrong way, into Stuart's lungs, and causing pneumonia. 'They're considering feeding him by tube, depending on what the speech therapist says. He's on a drip, too.' A drip would help prevent Stuart getting dehydrated. If he had problems swallowing, he wouldn't be able to drink enough, and dehydration could make the stroke worse.

'I'll come straight up after surgery finishes,' she said. 'Which ward are you on?'

'Stroke unit,' he said.

'OK. I'll see you then.'

Two quick calls after surgery reassured her that Robin and Sophie were fine at their friends' houses, then she drove to the hospital and walked up to the stroke unit.

Isabel and Oliver were sitting at either side of Stuart's bed. Nigel was conspicuous by his absence. Rachel noted that Stuart was asleep. She tapped lightly on the door and walked in.

'How is he?' she asked.

'As well as can be expected,' Isabel said. 'He's had a stroke.'

Rachel muffled her irritation. She had issues with Isabel that needed tackling, but now was definitely not the time for a confrontation with her mother-in-law. 'Oliver rang me earlier about the tests,' she said. 'Are they planning to give him any clot-busting drugs?'

'I did ask, but there isn't a trial here,' Oliver said.

Rachel nodded and sat down next to Isabel. 'Have you had anything to eat since this morning, Isabel?' she asked gently.

'How can I eat when my husband's lying here like this?' Isabel asked, seemingly affronted.

'You need to look after yourself, too,' Rachel said quietly. 'If you don't eat or rest you'll be ill, and Stuart needs you to be strong. Why don't you and Oliver go to the cafeteria?' She forestalled Isabel's protest by adding, 'I know you want to stay with him—of course you do, it's only natural—but he's asleep right now, and you do need a break. I'll stay with him. If anything happens, I'll come straight down and fetch you,' she promised.

'She's right,' Oliver agreed. 'And I need a comfort break.'

Only a Bedingfield would say that, Rachel thought. Anyone else would have said, 'I need the loo.'

'Back in a minute,' Oliver muttered, and left the room.

'Is Nigel coming this evening?' Rachel asked.

Isabel shook her head. 'He's on holiday.'

Rachel clearly wasn't quick enough to mask her thoughts, because Isabel bridled. 'It's not his fault.'

'No.' Just typical Nigel, not to leave a contact number. And even if they did manage to track him down, Rachel doubted that he'd offer to cut his holiday short and come home to support his mother.

'Don't you make judgements,' Isabel said.

'I'm sorry.' Rachel sighed. 'Look, I know I'm not the daughter-in-law you wanted, but right now I'm the only one you've got. We've had our differences, but in my family you're there when someone in your family needs you, regardless of what's happened over the years.'

Isabel still had her chin lifted high and her face turned away from Rachel. Rachel bit her lip. What would it take to reach Isabel? She'd spent fourteen years trying and failing. 'What I'm saying is, I'm here. And I'll do anything I can to help. If you'd like to stay with us while Stuart's here, I can soon freshen up the spare room for you.' Even though she knew that would mean Oliver would feel too awkward to make love, take comfort in her arms and reforge the bonds between them. 'And I can run you up here and fetch you again any time.'

This time Isabel turned to her, and Rachel was shocked to see that the older woman actually had tears in her eyes.

'Thank you,' she whispered.

Oliver appeared in the doorway. 'Do you want us to bring you anything back?' he asked Rachel.

She shook her head. Although she hadn't eaten, she wasn't hungry. 'I'm fine. See you in a bit.'

When they'd gone, she glanced over Stuart's charts—which showed that he was holding his own—and then settled down into the chair beside the sleeping man. 'It's such a mess, Stuart. None of this was ever meant to happen,' she said softly. 'Just when Oliver and I were starting to sort things out between us... But it's not your fault. You couldn't help it.' She sighed. 'All I know is that the next couple of days are going to be critical. For you and me both.'


'Where'm I?' Stuart mumbled a little while later.

'Stuart, it's Rachel.' She took his hand. 'You're here in hospital. Isabel and Oliver have gone to get something to eat. Do you want me to get them?'

'No. 'S all right.' Stuart's hand tightened on hers. 'Rachel. Need to tell you.'

'Shh, it's OK,' she soothed.

'Need to tell you,' he mumbled. 'Made a mistake. About you. Silly. You're right for Oliver.'

After all these years Stuart was finally telling her that he approved of her? Or was it that the stroke had scrambled some of his circuits and he was mixing her up with Caroline Prentiss?

'Great kids. Good mum. Ro— Ro—' He looked at her,

wide-eyed, clearly unable to remember the children's names.

'Robin and Sophie,' she said softly.

'Looks like you. The little one.' He looked anxious. 'Where's Oliver?'

Clearly the stroke had affected his short-term memory—she'd already told him that. 'In the cafeteria, with Isabel.'

'And the kids?'

She smiled. 'Robin's staying with his best friend, and Sophie's staying with hers. But I can bring them to see you tomorrow, if you like.'

He shook his head. 'Might scare them. Don't want to frighten them. Drip, tubes. Not nice for littlies.'

'You're probably right. But I know Madam will insist on making you a get-well-soon card. It'll be pink and purple.'

He smiled. ''S nice.' He took a shuddering breath. 'My chart?'

'Don't tell me you're going to live up to the stereotype and be a dreadful patient?' Rachel asked.

'You seen it?'

'Yes,' she admitted. 'And it looks OK.'

'Truth?'

'Truth,' she said. 'I wouldn't lie to you, Stuart.'

He smiled. 'You're tough. Need to be. Hard to be doctor and a parent.'

Was he trying to tell her that he thought Oliver was a workaholic, too?

'Harder now,' he added.

'We muddle through,' she said lightly. She and Oliver had stumbled into a quagmire, but she knew now that they'd find their way out again.

'Know you love Oliver.'

'Yes, I love Oliver. I've loved him for a very, very long time.' She willed the tears to stay back. 'Now, you're supposed to be resting. Isabel'll skin me if she thinks I've tired you out.'

'Tired.' He smiled wryly. 'Stroke.' Then he frowned, as if searching for the right word.

'You're right, tiredness is a common symptom afterwards,' Rachel supplied. 'And so is forgetting words. I know how annoying it must be, but it'll get easier, I promise.'

'Feel stupid.'

She smiled. 'You're very far from being that. You've probably forgotten more about medicine than I'll ever know.'

He drifted back to sleep again, still holding her hand. A few minutes later, Oliver and Isabel returned to the room.

'How is he?' Isabel asked.

'He woke briefly—I told him where you were and he was fine about it,' Rachel said, gently disengaging her hand from Stuart's and giving up her seat to her mother-in-law. 'Do you want me to pick you up later and bring you back to ours?'

'Thank you, but I've already arranged to stay here tonight,' Isabel said.

Rachel sighed inwardly. So much for thinking she'd had a minor breakthrough earlier. Isabel was as cool and distant as she'd always been. 'Fair enough. But if you change your mind, you're more than welcome.'

'You'd better get back to the children,' she said.

'Right. Oliver, are you staying here with your mother?'

'No, I'll come back with you,' he said. 'I need to arrange locum cover for tomorrow.'

'I'll see you tomorrow, Isabel,' she said.

'I'll ring if there are any changes,' Isabel said, and settled back in her chair next to Stuart.

\*     \*     \*

Oliver and Rachel walked slowly back to the car.

'I hope you're not blaming yourself,' Rachel said softly.

'Me?'

She refused to let him deflect the question. 'Are you?'

He sighed. 'If I'd taken the call…'

'He'd already had the stroke by then. It wouldn't have changed anything.' She squeezed his hand. 'You know, your dad thinks you work too hard.'

'My father said that?' Oliver shook his head, as if trying to clear it. 'All these years I've tried so hard to live up to his reputation. And now he doesn't even want me to.'

'That's not how he put it. He said it's harder now to do your job and be a parent, not like it was in his day. So if you're worrying that he's going to react badly to the changes you want to make, don't. He'll be fine about it.' She swallowed. 'He told me the kids were great. That he approved of me.'

'Rach, to know you is to love you.'

'Your mother doesn't.' She sucked in a shuddering breath. 'Sorry, sorry. I shouldn't land this on you. Not now.'

'We agreed we'd talk. Always,' Oliver reminded her. 'My mother's a difficult woman. But she's going to have to make a lot of adjustments now. She saw you holding my father's hand and talking to him—as a real person, not as someone who had to be humoured or pitied. Maybe she doesn't think she measures up to you, that she can't do the things that you can.'

'That's crazy.'

'Rach, people love you. I've heard them talk about you in the village. They think of you as *theirs*—whereas my mother's always been set apart. And the way you are with the kids…she was never like that with me. I don't think she knew how.' He shrugged. 'Maybe that's why I resented you being like that with them—because no one had ever been like that with me.'

'Oliver.' She held him tight. 'When we get home, when I've put the kids to bed—'

'When *I've* read their bedtime stories,' Oliver cut in.

'When they're asleep, I'll show you exactly how I feel about you. I love you, body and heart and soul. And nothing's ever going to change that.'

'Me, too,' Oliver whispered.

'We're going to get through this.'

'It's going to make us stronger,' Oliver said.

'And somehow I'll square things with your mother. I'll— Hell, I'll even learn the right accent, if it makes her happy.'

'No. Just be yourself,' Oliver said. 'My love, my wife.'

'Always,' she promised.

# EPILOGUE

*Fourteen months later*

OLIVER and Rachel stood on the balcony overlooking the Seine, his arms wrapped round her waist and his chin resting on her shoulder. 'Ten years. Doesn't seem like it, does it?'

'No.' She leaned back against him.

'I can still remember how you looked when you walked down the aisle towards me,' Oliver said. 'The most beautiful woman in the world.'

'I was convinced I'd trip over the hem of my dress and fall flat on my face. I was terrified.'

'You didn't look it. Just serene. And very, very beautiful.'

She smiled. 'Flattery will get you anywhere.'

'I hope so.' He rubbed his cheek against hers. 'Come with me, Dr Bedingfield,' he whispered.

She allowed him to waltz her back into their suite. The honeymoon suite—a surprise from Oliver to celebrate their tenth anniversary. Paris, as he'd planned for their first anniversary—except they'd never got round to it and had put it off. And, to her even greater surprise, he'd arranged for his parents to look after the children for the weekend.

Isabel had thawed a great deal over the last fourteen months. Probably at Stuart's prompting, Rachel thought. Since his recovery from the stroke, Stuart had become a lot closer to both Rachel and Oliver. And right at this moment Robin had probably found a quiet corner in his grandparents' house and had his nose in a book, whereas Sophie was likely to be bossing her grandfather into telling her another Princess Mouse story. And Caroline—who'd become good

182

friends with Rachel over the last year or so—was taking over for the day tomorrow to give Isabel a break and keep her sweet towards the children.

'Ten years. According to my mother, traditionally it's the tin anniversary,' Oliver said conversationally. 'So...' He took a neatly wrapped package from the drawer next to his side of the bed. 'Happy anniversary, love.'

She opened the parcel, and burst out laughing as she saw the can of pineapple. The first pudding she'd ever made for Oliver had been a pineapple upside-down cake, and if she didn't have time to make a pudding for dinner, she usually opened a tin of pineapple and served it with ice cream. 'Thank you.' She grinned. 'I wasn't expecting a present. You've already given me what I wanted most.' Time. A *lot* of time since he'd installed a practice manager and signed up the out-of-hours service. And Oliver was no longer missing out on all the children's milestones. He'd even taken over the bedtime story routine with Sophie.

'Well, it's traditional to give your wife an anniversary present. But I looked up the anniversary lists on the Internet. The modern list doesn't say it's tin.'

'No, it says it's diamond jewellery.'

'How do you...? Oh.' He grinned. 'You did the same.'

'Mmm-hmm. Great minds think alike.' She walked over to her bedside cabinet and extracted a small box. 'Happy anniversary.'

He opened the box. 'Wow. Cornish tin,' he said, looking more closely at the cufflinks. 'Thanks.'

'It met the traditional and the modern criteria,' she pointed out.

The tiny diamonds in the centre of the cufflinks gleamed in the light.

'And all I got you was a silly present. A tin of pineapple,' Oliver said ruefully.

'I don't need presents. I've got you.'

He kissed her. 'For always.'

She kissed him back. 'Definitely.'

'You know, I really fancy some pineapple.'

'What? Oliver, if you really want pineapple, we can call room service.'

'Not the same.' He raised an eyebrow at her. 'And we ought to use your present, don't you think?'

'Another day, maybe.'

'Now.'

She frowned. 'Oliver, what…?'

He handed her a tin-opener.

'But this is a hotel!' What was he doing with a tin-opener in a hotel—a posh hotel at that?

'So?'

She sighed. 'All right, all right. If you insist, I'll open the pineapple. But if I get juice all over the carpet and we get slapped with a cleaning bill, it's your fault.' She took the lid off the can, then stopped. 'What?' It was full of shredded tissue paper, not pineapple. 'How…?'

'You know Wayne Groves became an apprentice at Hollybridge Garage when he left school. Well, he was doing a welding course the other week,' Oliver explained. 'He, um, needed to do a bit of practising. And he thought he owed us a favour, since you spotted he had Weil's disease last summer.'

'You got Wayne to weld a tin of pineapple back together?'

'After I'd emptied it and washed it up. The kids helped.'

'They knew about this? No way. Sophie would've told me.' Sophie couldn't keep secrets—if she went to the supermarket with Oliver, she'd run in to Rachel to announce that Daddy had bought her some flowers.

'No, they just scoffed the pineapple.' Oliver grinned. 'I told Wayne what I wanted to do, so he put some metal in the bottom to make the tin feel the right weight.'

'You devious…' But she was smiling as she took out the tissue paper and discovered the tiny velvet-covered box. 'Oliver, it's beautiful,' she said, taking the diamond eternity ring out of the box, a band of flat-cut diamonds encircled by gold.

'And so are you, Rachel Bedingfield. I just wanted to say happy anniversary. And that I'll love you for ever.'

'Ditto,' she said. And she kissed him.

MILLS & BOON®

*Live the emotion*

# _MedicaL_
## romance™

### THE CELEBRITY DOCTOR'S PROPOSAL

*by Sarah Morgan*

When Dr Sam McKenna left his home town, he landed a prime-time TV slot. *Medical Matters* is top of the ratings! Now Sam has been roped in to be GP Anna Riggs's locum for the summer – and he's dragged his film crew along with him! Anna's furious – but then she realises that Sam's caring attitude is not simply a camera trick!

### UNDERCOVER AT CITY HOSPITAL

*by Carol Marinelli* (Police Surgeons)

Sexy ER consultant Heath Jameson catches Bella's eye instantly – but she knows she shouldn't get involved. She is a police officer, working undercover in the hospital to catch a drug thief, and she can't risk exposing her investigation. But Bella can still feel her life beginning to change, no matter how hard she tries to resist their mutual attraction…

### A MOTHER FOR HIS FAMILY *by Alison Roberts*

Nurse Sarah Mitchell wants to relax on her Fijian holiday. The last thing she wants is a fling with playboy Dr Ben Dawson. Until a cyclone hits the tropics and Sarah sees the true Ben – a talented surgeon with a big heart, a past, and a daughter in need of TLC. But Ben's attempts at love have hurt him before – can he trust his instincts again?

## On sale 1st July 2005

*Available at most branches of WHSmith, Tesco, ASDA, Martins, Borders, Eason, Sainsbury's and all good paperback bookshops.*

Visit www.millsandboon.co.uk

MILLS & BOON®

*Live the emotion*

0605/03b

# _MedicaL romance™

### A SPECIAL KIND OF CARING by *Jennifer Taylor*

Dr Francesca Goodwin wants to escape – from London, from the pain of her last relationship, from people. Working as a GP in isolated Teesdale sounds perfect – until she meets her new partner, Dr Alex Shepherd. He's good-looking, caring – and attracted to her!

### THE FLIGHT DOCTOR'S LIFELINE by *Laura Iding*

(Air Rescue)

Helicopter pilot Reese Jarvis is drawn to Dr Samantha Kearn from the moment he sees her in action with the Lifeline Medical Air Transport team. When he learns she is having trouble with her ex-husband, he immediately wants to protect her. He becomes her lifeline, her support – but ever since his fiancée died he has been reluctant to put his feelings on the line...

### THE BUSH DOCTOR'S RESCUE by *Leah Martyn*

Nurse Ally Inglis doesn't know why Dr Marc Ballantyne has come to the Outback town of Hillcrest, she's just grateful to have a full-time doctor at last. Marc charms and surprises everyone – not least of all Ally. He stirs up feelings she thought she'd never have again. But she can't help wondering, does this modern-day knight *really* mean to rescue her heart...?

## On sale 1st July 2005

*Available at most branches of WHSmith, Tesco, ASDA, Martins, Borders, Eason, Sainsbury's and all good paperback bookshops.*

*Visit www.millsandboon.co.uk*

MILLS & BOON

**Volume 12
on sale from
4th June
2005**

# Lynne
# Graham

## International Playboys

*Tempestuous*

*Reunion*